DragonFire

Book Two

Will of Fire

M. KATHERINE CLARK

Other Works by M. Katherine Clark

The Greene and Shields Files:
- Blood is Thicker Than Water
- Once Upon a Midnight Dreary
- Old Sins Cast Long Shadows
- Tales from the Heart, Novelettes

The Holmes Family Series
- Soundless Silence a Sherlock Holmes Novel
- The Rest is Silence, an Edmond Holmes Novel

Love Among the Shamrocks Collection:
- Under the Irish Sky
- Across the Irish Sea
- On the River Shannon
- The Land Across the Sea, an Emmet O'Quinn Short

Love Among the Shamrocks Collection,
        The Next Generation:
- In Dublin Fair City
- Song of Heart's Desire
- Chasing After Moonbeams – Coming Soon

The Wolf's Bane Saga:
- Wolf's Bane
- Lonely Moon
- Midnight Sky
- Star Crossed
- Moon Rise
- Moon Song, a Companion

DragonFire
- Heart of Fire
- Will of Fire

MacCulloch Castle Ghosts
- Silent Whispers, a Scottish Ghost Story
- Silent Night, a MacCulloch Castle Christmas – Coming Soon

For all those who believe in second chances and true love!

Prologue

Cahal

I stood watching the first of the Lewis Clan arrive on our lands. Only a fortnight had past since the battle that claimed my youngest brother's life and the other; Nameless. In honor of my father's decree, no dragon used the name of the second brother we lost. The traitor. He remained Nameless forevermore.

From my perch on the highest ledge of the mountain our castle was built into, I watched the caravan of loyal Lewis clan members, led by Rhys, the human warrior who had fought with us against the Lewis Laird. He stepped to the side when he arrived at the gate and once the gate was raised, he ushered everyone in, assisting some of the elderly and infirm. He was a good male. From the short time I watched him fight and then his wish to pledge his loyalty to my father, I kenned he would make a good addition to our clan, even though he was human.

Catching movement to my right, I looked over to see my sister-by-mating and future queen; Brigid step on to the ledge overlooking the clan. She looked out at the people below and wrapped her arms around herself. Even with the distance between us, I still caught the scent of my brother's essence within her. She carried his heir and with all the death around us the last couple weeks, it was good to have something to smile about. I watched her for a long while, seeing the emotionless look on her face. But soon, her heart began to beat furiously and suddenly, she burst into tears. My dragon roared wanting to know what threat hurt our future queen, but I knew nothing had happened and it had everything to do with the clan below. Her clan.

Crouching, I pushed off the perch and glided to the ledge where she stood. Immediately, she wiped her tears, not looking at me as I shifted and pulled on my plaid from the pouch tied at my ankle.

"What has you in tears, Brigid?" I asked, once decently clothed. She shook her head but even when I followed her gaze, I saw no one below who would warrant such tears. "Is all well with Finn?" I asked after my brother and her mate.

"Och, aye," she put my immediate nerves to rest. "I am being silly. It is the child."

"There is nothing silly about carrying the future heir," I said.

"Nay, of course no', but, what I meant was, when a woman carries a child, her emotions are heightened."

"Ah, forgive me, I did not know that," I needed to apologize for my assumption, but having never been around a female carrying a whelp except my mother who never showed any negative emotion, I did not know what she meant by being silly.

Brigid forced a smile. "It is all right, Cahal."

Over the last few weeks, I had attempted to show the real me to both Finn and Brigid. Since she had only known me as the moody, lurking, brother, I wasn't sure if I was making any progress.

"Should I leave you? Do you wish to be alone?" I asked.

She pressed her lips together and shook her head as her eyes filled with tears once more.

"Brigid, tell me what is hurting you and if it is within my power, I will destroy it."

She breathed a laugh and wiped her eyes. "You are very sweet," she said.

"Sweet?" I questioned. It was true I had a bit of a sweet tooth, but I was unsure why my occasional indulgence in minced pies and tablet had to do with my substance. I decided it was more human words I would not understand.

She smiled through her tears. "Aye, I am sorry I did nae realize it before."

"Is sweet a good thing? I have nae been around humans enough to ken."

"Aye, sweet is a very good thing," she confirmed. We were silent for a long moment until she sighed harshly. "Seeing all these people, my former clan, some were my friends, others my patients, but the two people I hope to see among them, I never will again."

"Who is that, lass?" I asked.

"My mother and father," she admitted. "They are dead."

"I had not been told the whole story," I tried to soften my

usually dark tone to offer comfort. "I am sorry for your loss."

"Thank you. I suppose carrying a child, I only wish to speak with my mother. I never got the chance to say goodbye and I need her now more than ever."

I nodded understanding at least that part. My brother, Bearcbhan had sought our da's council on more than one occasion, speaking to him of becoming a father and I was certain it was the same if not more so for a female.

Unable to say anything that would put her at ease, I simply followed her gaze to the bailey as Finn and Kai our War Chief, bustled around welcoming everyone and assisting them with their possessions. Finn had ordered the deserted cottages on the edge of our land to be fixed for the guests but tonight, there would be a feast welcoming them to MacKay lands, allowing those who desired to pledge their loyalty time to do so, and announcing Brigid's pregnancy.

I heard a young woman shout to Rhys and my eyes moved to the side door of the keep. The laird's widow and Brigid's friend, Cairstine ran out of the keep and into the arms of the young warrior who helped during the battle. They held each other tightly and when he pulled back, he kissed her firmly. My brows rose at such a blatant display of claiming his female but as a cheer rang out from the other clan members, it was clear the star-crossed lovers were favorites among their people.

Brigid smiled beside me as we watched. "Well," she said softly. "It looks like some good will come of this, after all." She turned to walk back into the keep. I bowed slightly to her as she passed me. Stopping a moment, she placed her hand on my arm.

"Thank you, Cahal," she said. "You protected me, and I never got a chance to thank you. Finn told me you landed on the balustrade on our wedding night because you feared Teyrnon... Nameless, may hurt me."

"I kept a close eye on you always, my future queen," I bowed again slightly. "It was my honor."

"Thank you, with all my heart." With that, she swept off the ledge and into the keep.

I turned back to the people below. One person in particular caught my eye. Sybine. My youngest brother's widow, but I couldn't forget what she was to me once... what we were to each other. The pain behind my chest flared and as I massaged the area, I continued to watch her as she helped the people. Keeping busy was always good medicine and Sybine needed a reprieve. I had tried to be there for my nephews, but I could not bring myself to approach their mother. She did not need me to give my condolences. She would be within her rights to not accept, given how I had treated her five years ago. But she had never been far from my thoughts.

The tight ball of pain spasmed in my chest once more and I knew the only way to stop it from growing would be to shift and fly. Doing just that, I leapt into the air and circled the bailey seeing females, whelps, and elderly males watching and pointing at me. They hadn't seen a dragon in a while, if ever for some of the younger ones. My eyes searched every face and made sure no threat entered our lands.

Sybine's eyes locked with mine and my dragon bowed his head toward her. She took a deep breath but lowered her eyes and moved to help another human.

Sybine

I felt someone's eyes on me, but I kept working not wanting to see who. Whoever it was had not stopped for a long while. I was assisting our new clan members as they entered the bailey. Keeping busy was all I could do, if I stopped even for a moment, I would fall to my knees and weep.

Bearcbhan had been gone for two weeks and every morning I still felt him kiss me awake but when I opened my eyes, he wasn't there. I couldn't count the tears I shed. Bearcbhan was a good male and I loved him. True, our story began as a mating of convenience, but he grew to become a male I admired and proudly proclaimed as my mate.

Shouting and squealing all around me broke me out of my thoughts. Looking to see what was wrong, I noticed all the humans were looking up and pointing. Lifting my eyes to the sky, I saw what had them so enthralled. Cahal's black dragon circled the bailey, watching. We locked eyes and he bowed his head toward me. As much as I appreciated what he had done, trying to save Bearcbhan in the battle with Nameless, seeing his dragon circle the bailey reminded me of that horrible day, five years ago when my life changed forever.

Chapter One

Sybine

Five years ago

Cahal was always so warm, but lying in the glen just beyond the front of the keep in the crook of his arm with the sun beating down on our skin he was deliciously fiery. Though it was not our first time together, every time with him was like the first time. His rough fingers threaded through my hair as I snuggled deeper into the crook of his neck, my fingers toying with the dusting of black wiry hair on his chest.

"I should be going," he said softly, kissing my hair.

"Mmm," I moaned. "Donnae leave yet."

"I must," he replied. "Da' is making the announcement later today."

"What announcement?" I asked. He froze against me. Raising my head, I looked down at him, but he would not look at me. "Cahal? What's going on?"

"Nothing," he hurried to say.

"Cahal," I pressed. "Tell me."

"I am... I entered the trials to be the War Chief."

"War Chief?" I breathed. "But War Chief is an unmatable position."

"Aye," he answered. "It is."

"And you entered without thought of me? Of us?"

"You ken this is what I have always wanted. Are you wanting to hold me back?"

I pushed off him in anger. "I want to mate with you." He couldn't be doing this. Not today. Not after... everything.

"And I wanted to mate with you too, but War Chief is an honorable position and one I am eligible for. My position as second born does not give me any chance of leadership. This is my only chance."

"And what about my chance? I gave you everything," I cried. "You swore you would mate me!"

"I never said that," he tried to justify. "Sybine, I do love you, but this may be my only chance."

So selfish. That's all he was. I should have known. I meant nothing to him. My virtue meant nothing to him. My future meant nothing to him. And the whelp I carried meant nothing to him. Grabbing my shift, I pulled it over my head, sick to my stomach. Cahal called my name but I did not look back.

Bearcbhan

The ta-do my father had planned for today was going to be boring so I snuck out through the back and into the gardens where I could leave to the beach and shift. As I breathed in the fresh air of freedom, I stopped when I heard a sob. Looking around, I did not see anyone but once I rounded the corner and looked through the archway of my mother's roses, I saw her. The beautiful Sybine. My brother's future mate.

She was weeping. Glancing back, Cahal was nowhere to be seen.

"Sybine," I called out. Immediately, she sniffled and wiped her tears. I strode forward and sat beside her on the stone bench. "Is something amiss? A female as beautiful as you should never be in tears."

"Please, go away, Bearcbhan," she said. "I want to be alone."

"I will go," I promised. "So long as you swear to me all is well." When she looked up at me, I was struck by her beautiful green eyes. She was so lovely, but I read sadness there. "What has happened?"

She sniffled, but soon a torrent of tears ran down her cheeks again. "Cahal," she gasped out. "Cahal has... he has petitioned to be War Chief."

9

What? That cannae be. Father would nae allow it. That is an unmateable position and surely he would not leave Sybine... *Oh gods, no.*

"He does not want to mate me," she cried. Immediately, I placed my arms around her slim shoulders and held her to me. We were the same age, but I could feel her grief as if it was my own. Damn him for treating such a lass the way he did. I know what she gave him and for him to toss her aside for a mere title was inexcusable.

"How could he do that to you?" She sobbed against me and my arms tightened around her. "I am so sorry, lass. I ken it does nae help but I am so sorry."

"What am I going to do? I gave him everything. The clan will shun me. I will never be able to mate. I am damaged. He swore he would mate me else I would never have..."

"I ken," I tried to soothe. "But you are not damaged. We will no' shun you. We are your family."

"No one will ever want me. The cast off of the prince."

Her bitterness crushed me, and I could not stop my next words. "I would."

She froze against me and I tried to bite back the words but couldn't. Finally, she pulled slightly away and looked up into my eyes. She was searching for something. I did not ken what.

"Why?" she finally asked.

"Why, what, lass?"

"Why would you want me?" she clarified.

I was not prepared for that question. How did I put it into words? I was not an eloquent male. I opened my mouth to speak but she stopped me.

"You know what it is I gave him." She flushed a deep red.

"Aye," I answered.

"And you still want me?"

"I donnae understand and never have; how it is acceptable for a male to do as he wishes and no' a female. You are held to such rigorous standards. Nay lass, I care not that you gave your innocents away. It was yours to give, no one's to take." I leaned my forehead toward her, but she pulled away and stood, her back to me.

"It is not only what I gave him," she paused and took a deep breath. "I believe I am carrying his whelp."

That took me off guard. I could handle the fact she was no' a virgin, most women I was with were not, but what surprised me was the horror she must be suffering. Carrying a whelp and alone, abandoned by the male who fathered the whelp.

I stood, after a moment of silence and walked over to her, pulling her to me gently.

"I am so sorry for all the strain you are under. Let me help with that burden? I am under no delusion you love me. Nor am I naive enough to think you will not always love him. I do nae want you to feel trapped but for your sake, and for the whelp, I want to help you. I care for you."

"You what?" She looked up at me with her innocent eyes surprised.

"I care for you. I always have. I stayed quiet as you were my brother's but now he has done what he has done. I am at liberty to speak. I care for you. And should you have me I swear to make you a good mate. I swear to take care of you. And make no designs on you until after the whelp is born. And this whelp,"

I covered her still flat stomach, "will be mine if you will have me. I would never force you, lass. I would hope one day you may grow to love me as well. If we were to mate, could you see yourself with me?"

I was trying to ask gently but dragons were very physical creatures, and I could never consign myself nor a potential mate to no physical love. She took a deep breath before she raised her head and brushed her lips against mine. In that moment, my dragon roared, and I held her to me giving her a taste of what she would have if she chose me. But I could not help and think I was getting the better end of the bargain. Her taste would have to sustain me a long nine months and beyond. As well as through my brother's challenge when we told my father of our mating. An angry Cahal was unpredictable and though he was not as strong as our eldest brother Finn, he was by far the best choice for War Chief. He could level entire villages with one gust of his powerful fire and a beat of his massive wings. To say I was scared of him was an exaggeration, but I was not looking forward to the battle and subsequent recovery, that was if he did not kill me.

Cahal

"We had many great candidates for War Chief and even though I am saddened that my dear friend decided to step down, I wish him health and happiness." Father stood on the raised dais in his best attire. Finn stood to his right and the old War Chief, my father's father's best friend sat to his left. The old male had been in the position for nearly sixty years and though the time had not been unkind, it was clear the male was ready to live out his days in peace.

My body still ached from the trials two days ago. Grueling was too kind a word. But it was nothing compared to the adrenaline coursing through me at the prospect I would be War Chief for my father and my brother, my best friend.

Finn grinned at me when I caught his eye. We were so very close in age we could almost have been twins but he was thirteen months older than me and closer than a brother. We fought well together, and I knew when he took over for Father we would lead the clan to a bright future.

Sybine's reaction troubled me. She knew this would be the best opportunity for me, but she was angry, I could tell. I was hoping to speak to my father after the ceremony. Perhaps, he could make an exception.

"The trials and games proved one dragon male among you is the best choice. As per tradition, he will have a day to think on his position and should he refuse the title, another among you will be chosen. Therefore, without further discussion. My son, Finn and I have agreed... Cahal, my son, join us up here as our new War Chief.

A sense of pride rushed through me as I heard my name and saw my father's smile. A grin spread across my face and my dragon preened in the back of my mind as the other males cheered. Taking the steps two at a time, I reached my father and brother who both greeted me with a warrior's shake.

"Congratulations, Brother," Finn stated with his rakish grin. "I look forward to our partnership."

"As do I," I said. "But I must speak to you both."

Father turned and gave the nod for the musicians to begin. The noise drowned out our conversation.

"What is on your mind, lad?" Father asked.

"I am so very thankful and grateful for this opportunity but, I beg of you, I want to mate with Sybine. I want to serve you and Finn as War Chief, it has been my greatest desire but... I cannae abandon Sybine. No' after what she gave me."

"You rogue," Finn chuckled.

"You ask me to strike down tradition for you to be able to marry the lass?" Da' asked.

"I love her," it was the first time I had said it out loud and for some reason it felt right. She was mine and I would fight for her.

"Dear me," father replied though I saw a twinkle in his eye. He turned to Finn. "What say you, son? He will be your chief."

"I say..." Finn paused, and I nearly punched his arm to get him to hurry up. "So long as he does not become weak and fat like so many males when they mate, I agree."

"Weak and fat?" My father echoed. "Better not let your mother hear you say that."

"I swear I will not, and I will always fulfill my duties before any other." Could they not give me a clear answer?

"Then Father, I have no issue with you... bending tradition," Finn said.

I turned to my father, my palms sweating. Father stared at me for a long time before his face split into a grin.

"It is granted, son. Go claim your mate and bring her back here so I may announce a mating in two days' time."

My heart soared. My beast roared inside my head. We would claim her before the others. We would have her. She would be ours.

"Da'!" Bearcbhan's voice came from the front. We all turned and even the musicians stopped playing. My world tilted on its head when I saw Sybine, my mate, clutching my brother's hand and hurrying behind him. All eyes followed them, I even felt Finn step up closer to me as if ready to defend my claim.

They stopped and bowed before my father.

"Bearcbhan, Sybine, what has happened?" Da' asked.

"The greatest thing, Da'," he said clutching Sybine's hand. "This beautiful female has agreed to be my mate. We desire you to mate us as soon as possible."

"What?" I bellowed. I never raised my voice but in that moment my dragon shouted so loudly inside my head it was the only sound I could hear.

The crowd before me silenced as all eyes turned to me.

"What is going on?" My father asked calmly. My eyes never left Sybine, but she did not raise her gaze to me. "Sybine? My dear?" Father continued.

She finally looked up at my father, raised her chin and took a deep breath.

"It is my choice, my king," Sybine said. "Bearcbhan is the most honorable, loving, and caring male of my acquaintance. And since I am unspoken for and free to do as I will, I have chosen Bearcbhan as my mate. Please, I ask for your blessing."

"Sybine," my father sighed. I felt his eyes on me for a moment. Then he looked back at my traitorous mate. I could not speak. My ears rang. My world was crumbling. "Sybine," my father said softly. "Come here, lass."

I saw her clutch Bearcbhan's hand, and I could not hold in my dragon. He took over my human form, my eyes slitting to the dragon within me.

"Leave her, you bastard!" my dragon shouted. Bearcbhan's eyes flashed to dragon slits but before he could say anything da' snapped.

"Cahal!" I looked over to see Da's eyes slitted too. "I ken you are upset but I will nae have you disparaging your mother by calling your brother a bastard."

My body shook and though I could see all that was happening I could do nothing to stop it. My dragon roared and in a moment, I was in my dragon form. Releasing my fire, I called for a challenge. I would challenge him, my brother, for my betrothed.

Sybine

Seeing Cahal so upset gave me pause. Perhaps he did care for me but then his words from that morning came back to me. He wanted more than anything to be War Chief and from the celebrations we heard when we came in, he had been given what he wanted. But still, seeing him so angry gave my dragon a moment's hesitation until I realized if I denied Bearcbhan and went back to Cahal, I would be deemed a whore and quite possibly shunned for pitting brother against brother. Then of course there was Cahal, he would never take me back now. Not after what I did. When my king asked me to his side, it was instinct to clutch Bearcbhan's hand. But as soon as Cahal saw it, his dragon took over and he shifted. His majestic black dragon blew out his fire and called for a challenge. He would kill his brother and it was my fault. Though I only just saw the goodness in Bearcbhan, I could not allow him to die for me.

"Enough!" I shouted. Feeling the tension radiate through

Bearcbhan, I knew he would shift. His honor had been questioned and he would avenge. "It is my choice who I mate. You have all you desire. You are War Chief. You cannae mate. And you told me today you care naught for me. Why would you condemn me to a life of loneliness? I will mate who I damn well please and you cannae naysay. He is more honorable than you could ever be. Not after all I gave you did you care once for me! I renounce you, Cahal as you renounced me by participating in the trials without telling me and as you renounced me this morning. Leave us in peace!"

Cahal blew out more fire hotter than ever. Bearcbhan could not ignore the challenge again. He glanced back at me and nodded. As a show of dominance, he kissed me for all to see but in that moment, he was torn from me by black claws and thrown out of the cave to land on his stomach. He lay still for a moment then slowly stirred as Cahal flew high into the sky and began to dive. Bearcbhan shook his head to clear it. His gaze landed on his brother's dragon and in less time than I could scream, he shifted into his golden dragon, rolling away from Cahal's deadly claws. As soon as Cahal dipped and missed, he climbed higher and let out a fearsome roar. Bearcbhan sat back on his haunches and beat his wings a few times to prepare and then he jumped.

Beating his wings again he climbed into the sky. Cahal hovered, waiting. They faced each other. Bearcbhan's size much smaller than Cahal's but they flew at each other and my heart seized. All of that simply because he wanted to be War Chief.

I felt my king and prince walk up beside me.

"Damn fools," Finn cursed watching.

"Please stop them!" I begged.

"I fly up there now and they may kill not only me but each other," Finn said.

"Not even my command will stop him, lass. You must tell me what happened," Edan stated from my side.

"It is as I said. He is your War Chief. He is unmatable," I justified.

"He petitioned me to strike down that rule. He was on his way to find you when you came in."

My heart lurched and my stomach twisted. Without a moment's pause, I vomited in the grass beside us. *What have I done?*

Cahal

I knew my dragon was out for blood, but I could not stop him. Anger coursed through me as my whoreson of a brother fought me. Whether it was my dragon's anger or mine, I did nae ken.

Soon, I saw my brother tire. My dragon took his chance and barreled into his chest. Bearcbhan made no noise when I dug my claws into the soft hide under his arms. His breath had been knocked out of him. I scented blood and satisfaction flooded my dragon. I heard a scream from somewhere below us.

Good, my dragon thought. *Let her suffer seeing her lover die. She will never betray us again.*

That gave me pause.

You would kill him? Our brother? I questioned my dragon.

He is no brother of mine.

He is. And if that did not get through to him, I tried another tactic. *He is our mother's and father's child.* I felt the hesitation in my dragon's body as he smelled more blood.

He stole our mate. My dragon spat.

As difficult as it was for me to say it, I charged ahead. *He did not. We left our mate alone. She meant everything to us and we left her. She gave us her most precious gift and we left her alone. What did we expect her to do? She would have been shunned. Cast out. Disgraced.*

But Father gave his permission.

But she did not ken that. Would you begrudge her a chance? Think. My heart is breaking just as much as yours, but it is the best way, I reasoned.

You would not fight for her? He growled.

I would give her what we could not have.

My dragon fell silent. I felt the moment his heart shattered. The pain was so great, I cried out and my dragon roared. I had never felt that kind of pain before, even in battle. I could not catch my breath. Looking down at her, I saw the sadness, pain and fear in her eyes. *What have I done?*

Immediately, I took control back from my dragon as he retreated to the back of my mind and sobbed. Releasing my brother, the dragon cried out and pushed away from me. I coasted back on my wings, looked at Bearcbhan. The male would be my female's mate and would be a father to her whelps.

Our gazes met and though I read pain in his eyes, there was also pride, he would never back down. He waited on me to make a move but one look down at Sybine, she looked pale and slight beside my brother and father.

One last look, I tried to tell her how sorry I was, but my dragon merely sobbed. I felt the tears seep down my hide.

Closing my eyes for a moment, I held on to the image of seeing her come alive with my touch. Then, looking back at my brother, I bowed my head and conceded the battle. With a final breath, I pushed my dragon higher and higher until I broke the clouds. I used to fly that high but had not for a long time. The sun shone brightly on my face and I prayed it would burn the memory away. I prayed it would burn the hurt.

How could I survive when my true mate chose another? How did I never tell her... I could see her dragon behind her eyes.

Chapter Two

Sybine

Five years later

I stared at my king in disbelief. "What are you saying?"

He sighed and took my hand in his rough one. "You ken what I am saying, lass."

"You cannae mean it," I replied, pulling my hand back

from him.

"No one is more upset and hurt by our laws than I am right now, Sybine," Edan answered. "And never would I have ever dreamed my last act as king would be to command my son's widow to marry again, three months after his death. Alas, as fate and the gods have it, it is. So, I ask for all eligible males to step forward. Sybine, you must choose your mate."

"My mate is dead," I cried looking at the six males who stepped forward. "You would ask me to defile my mate's memory by taking another to my bed before he is even cold? Before he is mourned properly?"

"You know no one here would force you to forget him. But our laws—"

"Damn the laws," I shouted.

"Do not do this," Finn stepped forward and spoke to me. "Do not make my father's last act and my first act as king be to banish you from our clan. No one wants that. We all love you, Sybine and we all loved Bearcbhan. I believe I speak on behalf of all males here when I say they would never force you and would allow you to mourn my brother."

"I cannae even think of being intimate with anyone. My mate just died!"

"Enough," Cahal shouted. Everyone went silent and he stepped forward. "I claim you as mate, Sybine. You are mine. Do you accept me?"

I stared at him for the longest time, fear caused my mouth to stop working. Eventually, the king stepped to my side and whispered, "you must respond. Please, Sybine. There are no greater males than my sons and Cahal tried to save him and did save Finn and Brigid. Do not let me see you be forced out, love.

Please, it would be like having to see my own daughter leave."

"I ask you again, Sybine," Cahal started. "Do you accept my mate claim?"

Swallowing away the lump in my throat, I remember how many years I had loved him. How many times had we promised to be together? The times he had made love to me. The horrible day we separated. And the unbearable day I found out, only a few days after I mated Bearcbhan that I was not carrying a whelp after all. All my fears were unjustified. But Bearcbhan, true to his word, let me acclimate to him being my mate before we consummated our mating. After that moment, I was happy. But when Cahal returned several weeks later, his position of War Chief had gone to Kai. He was never the same.

"Sybine," Edan urged. "Please." My eyes never left Cahal's, his hand still extended toward me.

Instinct took over and oddly my dragon was quiet. I finally nodded.

"Say it out loud, lass," the king pressed.

"Aye," I squeaked. "I accept your claim."

Cahal's expression never faltered but his eyes flashed to dragon slits and then back.

"Take your mate's hand and stand before me, Sybine."

With my back, ramrod straight, I stepped down and took Cahal's hand. A shiver ran down my back and I gasped. Cahal did not react but took my hand in his strong embrace and stood before his father.

The mating ceremony went by in a blur. I did not know what was said but when I felt the black onyx stone ring, Cahal's claim, slip onto my finger, and the king announce we were mated, I went through the motions. When I turned to look at my new mate, my most incriminating secret shown clear as day behind his eyes. I could see his dragon... and I could never see Bearcbhan's.

Cahal

She was mine. Finally. Mine. I thought it would feel differently, but knowing she was my brother's widow cooled the flame that still burned hotly for her. I always wanted her. For a time, I wondered if the twins were mine, but the timing did not work. They were clearly Bearcbhan's, but for the longest time I wondered why she was so quick to mate. Shaking my head, I cleared it. It did not matter. She was mine now, but unlike the other voracious males near us, I would give her the proper time to mourn my brother. As annoying as my youngest brother was, and even though he betrayed me, I still needed time to mourn him.

But now, the clan required a kiss. Hopefully, they would be satisfied knowing our history. I leaned down and, forcing my dragon into the back of my mind, I kissed her lightly. It did little good. My dragon recognized his mate and roared, racing to the forefront of my mind to claim her properly. It was all I could do to stop him. The pain was nearly unbearable, but I tore my mouth away from hers and took three steps back.

"By dragon fire you are one!" My father shouted. The clan roared and I blew out the traditional fire, my dragon producing the scales to protect my human throat. Sybine didn't look at me. She had gone pale and trembled, but I stood beside her to help in any way I could.

"The mating ceremony is complete. I am officially

handing my title to my first-born son Aodhfionn. He has proven himself to be a good and loyal leader. As always but especially in these last couple months since my youngest son died, Aodhfionn has shown he is the best choice to succeed me. With his mate by his side, he will lead this clan as its king. I still intend to be near but will no longer be leading the clan. I ask you all to pledge your loyalty to my son and his mate as your new king and queen." Da' spoke in his usual commanding tone. As his only surviving brother... that thought struck me out of the blue, I was the first to kneel and withdraw my dirk. Seeing my elder brother step forward and my father step back, was a surreal moment. Ever since I was a child, I knew my brother would be king, but as I knelt pledging my loyalty, I could not help but smile. It was foreign to me, but it felt... right.

Finn took a deep breath and pulled himself up to his full height.

"It is my honor to be named king. I will strive to emulate my father's teachings and expertise. He is truly the best male I know. One thing he has taught me is, anything is possible with the right female by my side." He turned and reached for his mate. Brigid was just starting to show at what we expect was five months pregnant. Brigid took his hand and stood beside him. "I have just that female by my side. My queen and I will lead justly and will take all of you into account when we make decisions. A king is only so good as the advisors who counsel him. I am very pleased to say I will be maintaining my father's current support but am adding one. Brother," I looked up. "I ask you join me as my most trusted advisor. In my absence you will lead. If you accept."

In that moment, we were close again. I had missed him. My closest friend was again by my side and I by his. Taking a deep breath, I nodded. "It would be my honor, my king."

"Then join me at my right."

I stood to join him but instantly felt Sybine fall into me. Clutching her, I shouted for a healer as I realized she had fainted.

Sybine

I was mated. It had all happened so fast I did not have time to process but as Cahal rose to his feet gently pulling me with him, my legs gave out and I fainted. The next thing I remembered, I was in my room and a cool linen was pressed to my forehead. Slowly opening my eyes, I looked over to see my sister-by-mating, the clan healer and new queen.

"Brigid?" I whispered.

"Shh, you are well." She leaned over me checking my eyes for something. Her five-month pregnant belly brushing my arm.

"What happened?" I asked.

"You fainted and Cahal carried you here," she explained in the matter-of-fact way I liked. As a female, but most importantly as a mother, I preferred to know what was happening without dealing with flowery language.

"Where are my whelps?" The youngest was still nursing and if the pain in my breasts was any indication, it was time for her to feed.

"Your boys are with Edan and your wee girl is with the clan nursemaid."

I nodded. They were well and I could rest. My head pounded and my dragon was trying to sleep to help me, but nothing helped. To distract from my thoughts, I turned to her.

"I suppose I should be bowing to you instead of you tending my sick bed."

"You are I are friends," she replied. "I donnae want you to bow to me."

"In private, I'll agree but in public, you are our queen," I countered.

"And you are the wife of my husband's most trusted advisor. But I'll also need someone to help me know what to do. Erina has given her counsel which I appreciate but I do not want to tire her with my questions."

"You would not," I encouraged, but her words brought back the fact I was mated again and I turned away.

"Oh come now," Brigid cooed. "It is not all bad, is it? Cahal is a good male."

"'Tis no' that," I replied.

"Then what is it?"

I couldn't tell her. Fortunately, I was saved by someone knocking on the door. Brigid walked over and opened it. From where I lay, I could not see who it was, but I would always know that voice.

"Is she well?" Cahal asked.

"Aye, she is awake," Brigid replied and stepped aside. Cahal entered the room and I tried to prevent my body from stiffening. Forcing my mind to remember he was my mate my husband, and I would be expected to share his bed that evening, I tried to find an excuse to postpone the inevitable.

His dark eyes found me, and I forced my gaze to meet his. We knew each other intimately but I was still nervous.

"I'll leave you both," Brigid said. I wanted to scream for her to remain, but I could not make my voice work. When the door closed behind her and we were alone, silence descended. Cahal stared at me for a long moment before dropping his gaze and pacing to the fire, lit with a black flame tinged with white. Cahal's fire. Never had a black flame lit Bearcbhan's and my hearth. It was either my iridescent or Bearcbhan's yellow.

"I thank you for carrying me back to my room," I said. "I am sorry for fainting, 'tis unlike me."

"Aye, I ken it," he spoke low. Of course he knew, he knew everything about me. "But," he shrugged. "'Tis to be expected."

We were quiet as I stared at his back. The broad muscular back that always made me feel safe when he held me. Finally, he huffed a sigh, turned, stared at me, and bowed slightly.

"I am glad you are well," he began. "Forgive me, I..." he said no more, only bowed once more and left the room quickly.

Chapter Three

Cahal

It had been so long since I had held her. Catching her when she sagged against me, had been second nature, but it also stirred my dragon. He demanded we take her somewhere safe and make her ours. Cover her in our scent and give her our whelp. Pushing my dragon to the farthest reaches of my mind and getting a short reprieve from his incessant need, I had looked over at Finn who had still stood on the dais. Finn nodded for me to take her back to her room and Brigid stepped forward escorting me to Sybine's chamber. Though we were mated, we had yet to consummate our union and as custom dictated, she could not be in my room yet.

Pacing outside her chamber, I waited to hear her voice. When I did, relief stronger than I would like to admit flooded my veins. I tried to stop myself from knocking but I could not. She needed to know I was there, and I needed to know she was well.

When as I left the room after speaking with her, my dragon burst forth from the back of my mind and would not stop roaring at me. I pushed myself to walk down the stairs and out the back door. My head pounded but I kept going.

"Cahal?" Finn called to me. I saw him standing on the bank of the loch. Though my dragon was going to burst forth soon, he knew his duty in giving our king the respect he deserved.

"Brother," I said through clenched teeth. "Forgive me, but my dragon is close to the surface."

Finn nodded. "Brigid had some pain earlier and my dragon needs to hunt. Care to join me?"

The thought of my sister-by-mating, my queen, having pain with her whelp worried my dragon enough, he calmed slightly.

"Is she well?" I asked.

"Aye, she claims it is nothing but growing pains, but my dragon does not like it."

"I do understand. She looked well when I saw her in Sybine's room."

"Aye, she refuses to rest," Finn huffed. "What our mates are putting us through…" he shook his head.

Our mates. My dragon roared so loudly, I winced.

"His need to claim?" Finn asked.

"Aye, but I will nae, no' until the proper time."

"I commend you. It is difficult."

"We are our father's sons," I replied. "We can resist."

"Aye, but it causes a bloody terrible headache," Finn said.

"That it does," I agreed.

"You ken what helped me those early days?" Finn prompted. I shook my head. "Hunting and flying. Let the beast out."

"Aye," I replied. "I plan on it."

"Might I join you?"

"You are king now, Finn," I lowered my eyes in respect. "Are you certain it is safe?"

"I will be with my most trusted advisor."

"And your War Chief." I heard Kai say from behind us. Finn and I turned to him as he walked up and bowed to my brother. "Do not think I donnae ken exactly where you are at all times, my king."

"Were you this possessive of my father?" Finn asked.

"Aye," Kai answered. "But his majesty knew better than to sneak away without telling anyone."

I growled. "Be careful, dragon. Know your place and to whom you speak." I felt Finn's hand on my shoulder.

"I thank you, brother," he said. "But 'tis glad I am you both are here for I wish to tell you. We grew up together. When we are alone, I will not forget that, and I ask you not forget it either. If I need a kick in the arse, I expect you both to do the kicking. You have my word if you feel the need to speak to me in a way you would a friend, then I expect you to do so without fear of reprisals. However, if we are not alone, I would expect you to hold your tongue even though we are friends. Among others, I am king."

Both Kai and I bowed to him in agreement.

"Now," Finn continued. "If you lads think you can keep up," the twinkle in his eyes made us laugh. "Let's go."

We shifted quickly and leapt into the air, flanking our king. Finn was only teasing when he said to *keep up*. He knew he was needed and could not fly on his own. The Lewis threat had been resolved at great loss to us all. But not all threats were over. Bearcbhan's face flashed before my eyes. There was no possibility I would force Sybine that evening, even if my dragon wanted her so badly I ached.

Finn gave a small roar just to get our attention. Looking over at him, he winked and dived, only to come back up behind us. It was the first move of an old game we used to play as lads. It was wonderful to be back with my dearest friends playing the games we all loved. We played for several minutes, it felt good to let the stress go and be a boy again. Finally, we were all exhausted and Finn clenched his back talon saying *let's stop.* Then he lifted his tail in a typical hunter's move saying there were stags nearby. I could smell them too. Getting in position, we dived to a small island.

The sun was slowly slipping below the mountains as we lounged in human form. Instead of eating the stags as dragons, we decided to do something we had not done for a long time. Build a fire, roast the deer, and simply talk.

I sat on a fallen log basting the meat over Kai's blue flame. Finn lounged on his side taking a drink from Kai's flask. Kai sat on a rock carving a piece of wood.

"I donnae ken where you had this, my friend but I am verra glad you did." Finn indicated the flask.

"I donnae ken what it is you both are going through, but I am glad it has helped," Kai grinned.

"When you mate you will," Finn replied.

"Aye," I replied gruffly. "Sometimes I wonder if females are truly worth it. They take hold of our bollocks and use them against us."

Finn nodded. "But then the thought of not having my warm, soft, willing lass in my bed comes to mind and I would gladly hand over my bollocks in a moment." Chuckling, he turned to Kai, oddly quiet and kicked his booted foot. "When is your turn, Kai?"

"Any female willing to mate him must understand his randy ways," I teased. "He needs a wanton willing to do all sorts of debauched things. No one of our acquaintance I bet," I winked.

He said nothing, odd for him, usually he would give back as good as he had but when I saw him pale, I wondered.

"Well... considering it is bound to be our sister, Cahal, I doubt we have little choice in the matter," Finn stated. I looked over at him surprised.

"What?" I questioned.

Kai hissed when the knife slipped and cut his thumb deeply. As Kai sucked on the wound, I locked eyes with Finn. My brows furrowed. He shook his head but when Kai stood, he looked over at him.

"I am going to find some fresh water to clean this. I will return shortly," he said though his wound had doubtless closed and healed by then. Once he was gone, I scooted closer to Finn.

"What on earth was that about?" I asked. Finn took a swig of whisky from the flask and looked over at me.

"Apparently Kai is our sister's true mate."

"What?" Had I been so focused on Teyrnon's betrayal I failed to see anything else around me? My eyes shot to where Kai had left the camp. "She is a child."

"She turned nineteen summers a moon cycle ago," Finn stated. "But I agree with you."

"He is nearly thirty!" I exclaimed.

"He's twenty-five, brother, a year younger than you."

"Not in experience," I replied.

"I agree, but da' and I have spoken with him. He claims to love her, and I will not prevent any from having their true mate. He swears certain... issues we have seen in the past are not something Tahra will need to worry about nor something we will ever hear of again."

"And you trust him?"

"I do."

I huffed. "I have much to learn after my many months away."

"Where were you?" Finn asked passing the flask to me.

"When I heard Nameless boasting about his plot, I knew what needed to be done."

"I need to know the whole story, from the beginning, Cahal."

Huffing a sigh, I nodded but took a hefty swig from the flask. "It was one evening Nameless and I went to the village for our... physical needs. I sat at one of the tables having my dinner before taking any lass to bed. Nameless had grabbed one of the human females offering herself to him and she sat on his lap. Though we came in together, we usually sat separately but near enough if we needed each other. Anyway, she was saying all the flowery things our brother was susceptible to and he wanted, I guess, to prove his prowess. He was speaking loudly as if intoxicated. But I overheard his plan and the agreement he had with the Lewis Chief. He said he would convince you to take the human lass and when they were sure she was carrying your whelp they would attack and force you to come after her, killing you in the process then blame me for it. He didn't realize I could hear him. In that moment, I knew the only way to stop him was to constantly monitor him and come up with a plan. Whenever he left, I followed. I also had to make you all believe it was me so Teyrnon would think his plan was perfect. My only regret is, I wasn't able to save Bearcbhan."

Finn said nothing as he stared straight ahead, not looking at me. Finally, he spoke.

"Our brother was troubled," was all he said. When he heard Kai approach, he lowered his voice. "'Tis glad I am you overheard his plan. Brigid and I... and our whelp are indebted to you."

Kai returned to the glow of the fire and for the first time, I looked at him as the male my sister apparently admired. Truly, she could have chosen worse. Kai was a strong warrior, a good male, loyal. My greatest concern was his physical experience. His needs and desires were... unique. But my conversation with Finn eased my fears. However, Kai and I would be speaking, alone.

I was glad we could put everything aside and enjoy the afternoon. Night waned fast on our island and I knew I needed to return to Sybine. I would never do anything to disgrace her before the clan and not showing on our wedding night would be the greatest disgrace.

Finn looked anxious to return to Brigid. Kai must have felt the charged air and soon, the fire was out, and we were shifting. We landed at the back entrance of the keep where we departed from earlier. Father met us with a glad smile and once we were shifted and dressed, he spoke to me.

"We were unsure if you would join us tonight."

"Aye, we merely needed to let our dragons out." I answered walking up the steps. Da' stopped me with a hand on my chest.

"The males are clamoring for their bedding ceremony," he whispered. "Some Lewis men have joined in too."

My eyes widened. "What? Why? She is nae a virgin."

"Aye, but it is still a mating."

"Nay. She is nervous enough as it is, I will nae subject her to that degradation," I stated.

"Unpleasant, isn't it, brother," Finn's jab was well deserved but I ignored it.

"I ask you to speak to them, da'," I begged.

"I am nae king," Da' said looking at Finn. I closed my eyes

for a moment. Finn had every right to tell me to go ahead with the tradition after what I put him through with his mating night with Brigid. But, praying harder than I had before and hoping our new friendship and our conversation earlier would serve to distract him. I turned, begging with my eyes. Finn paused as if thinking then, fighting a smile, he said the same words to me he said on his wedding night.

"'Tis an antiquated ceremony for old men and bastards who get their jollies from watching a poor innocent girl be taken advantage of. I say, if they cannae get their own into their bed donnae try and watch ours." I breathed a sigh of relief when Finn winked. "A little reciprocation is good for the soul, brother."

"You may have as much as you please, Finn and I thank you."

He thumped my back. "I will say, you must choose where you are to sleep. Your dragon has already tasted what she has to offer. You may need to find a way to prevent your dragon from taking over."

I had not thought of that. My dragon and I were one but the moment he sensed his mate, I would be hard pressed to prevent him from taking over my body and taking what he wanted. My dragon sat in a huff and spoke low.

I would never hurt her. Nor force her. She is ours. Our mate. As much as I do want her, I will wait.

"He will wait. He loves her," I confirmed.

"If you are unsure when he catches her scent," Da' started and pulled out a small vial. Pressing it into my hand, he locked eyes with me. "A derivative of Dragon Bane. It will put your dragon to sleep in the back of your mind." Nodding, I thanked him.

"Slip up the back stair," Finn instructed. "I will distract the men. Kai, will you assist me?"

"Aye, my king," he replied. Finn raised an eyebrow but prevented his chuckle as he passed our father, squeezing his arm in affection.

Once we were alone, I spoke to da'. "Did I do the right thing?"

"Do you doubt it?" he questioned.

"Aye," I sighed. "I fear she will always hate me for choosing title over her."

"But you did not," Da' said. "You wanted both. There is nae shame in that. Your brother and Sybine acted rashly. Donnae hold that in your heart. You did what anyone who loves her would have done. You protected her from others who perhaps would not have treated her with the respect a grieving widow deserves."

I nodded. I should have known da' knew my plan. I would not mate with her in truth until she asked. Before I went up the back stairs, I looked back to the loch, its small waves were a tune I loved both grown male and boy. Taking a deep breath of the deep salty air, I held it in my chest and closed my eyes.

"What else preys on your mind, son?" Da' asked. I looked into da's dark eyes. He seemed to have aged the last few months and immediately I wanted to tell him how sorry I was for the loss of not only one, but two sons.

"I am so sorry, da'," I said. My voice catching as all of the events and tragedies of the last three months came back to me. "I tried to stop him, but I wasn't fast enough." I did not realize tears slid down my cheeks until my father cupped my face and I felt the wetness. Seeing mirroring tears swimming in his dark depths, my heart hurt. He pulled me into him and held me tightly.

"My son," he whispered, his voice rough. "I love you. You are not to blame. You saved Finn and the entire clan. Myself, included." Kissing my cheek, he thumped me on the back and tightened his hold on me for a moment then pulled back. "Now, get you upstairs and into your chamber. Though I know you will abstain, your lass awaits. Put her at ease, Cahal. She has been through more than anyone of her young age should have."

Nodding once, I said goodnight and hurried up the back stairs to my room. Pausing a moment before my door, I raised my hand to knock but could not bring myself to lower my knuckles. Taking a deep breath, I closed my eyes and spoke low.

"Brother, Bearcbhan, I do this in honor of you. I ken you loved her. I never wanted this to happen. If I could change places with you, I would. But know this, I will take care of your whelps. Your mate will always mourn you, but I do ask for your blessing. Give me a sign." Hauntingly, at that moment, I heard my brother's laughter. Turning toward the sound, his apparition stood by the stairs. He winked at me and disappeared. Blinking, wondering if Kai had something other than whisky in his flask, I shook my head, but it felt like a weight had been lifted off me. Raising my hand once more, I knocked with more confidence than I expected.

Sybine

When I was feeling better, Brigid, Erina, and Tahra came to sit with me. I apologized for the foolish way I handled the ceremony, but they all brushed it off as if saying it was to be expected. I had not seen Cahal since he came to check on me.

Once, we had a knock on the door, it was Edan looking for his wife. But when asked about Cahal, he merely shrugged. I wasn't sure what to make of that. As the sun slowly slipped behind the mountain, I wondered if I would see my new mate that evening. Brigid looked tired and uncomfortable.

"The child is particularly active tonight," she said stroking her belly.

"He is growing and needs room," Erina smiled patting her hand.

"Aye, grow into a strong lad, little one," Brigid spoke to her belly. I remembered what it was like carrying my whelps. The weight was exorbitant with twins, but I would not trade them for anything. The last three months the healer watched them closely after their beatings at the hands of the Lewis and when they both shifted the first time after the attack relief like never before swept over all of us. They asked where their father was. I tried to tell them, but they were so young they did not understand. Finn and Cahal were godsends playing with their nephews and distracting them.

"Perhaps we should get you ready, dear," Erina said to me, seeing the darkness growing. "I am sure the males will return soon."

"Where did my husband get himself to?" Brigid asked.

"According to Edan, he saw Kai, Finn, and Cahal fly west to the island."

"Kai was with them?" Tahra asked.

"Aye, dear, he is War Chief, his place is by Finn's side."

"I am surprised Kai was War Chief. I would have thought it would be one of his brothers," Brigid said.

I felt sick. Of course she did not know but I did not think I could rehash all of it. Silence descended and Brigid looked at each of us.

"Oh..." she said. "I am sorry. I have tread into murky waters, haven't I?"

"No need to be sorry, dear," Erina said. "But perhaps it is a tale better left for later."

Brigid nodded and said no more. "Now, let us get you prepared."

"I donnae think I can do this," I said softly.

Erina knelt before me and took my hands. She did not say anything until I looked into her eyes.

"Cahal would never ask it of you. He desires you, that much is clear, but knowing him as his mother, I can assure you he will make no designs on you. But you are within your rights to refuse him."

"He is my mate. He has rights too."

"Aye, but you are within yours in the customs of our clan to refuse any male, husband or no'."

Taking a deep breath, I nodded but stood letting the women assist me.

Having seen my whelps earlier that day, I was able to nurse my daughter and listen to my sons. Their playful nature helped me relax. But as Erina pulled out a beautiful linen night dress, my eyes filled with tears. The ladies helped me dress saying nothing and then took their leave. Only Erina stayed behind.

She did not say anything only walked to the side desk and poured two glasses of wine. Coming back to me, she handed one and drank from the other. Forcing me to have a drink, the wine calmed my stomach but not my mind.

"I ken you loved Bearcbhan and I, along with my husband, hated what you were forced to do today but as you ken, you loved Cahal once. I ask you hold on to that tonight and believe in his goodness. He loves you and he mourns his brother too." I nodded just as there was a sharp knock on the door. And just like that, my nerves returned.

Cahal

When my mother answered the door, she smiled softly but held up a hand warning me.

"She is extremely nervous," she said so softly I doubt even Sybine's dragon could hear. I nodded but replied,

"The males want their bedding ceremony. Finn and Kai have gone to distract them."

I heard a gasp and realized Sybine had heard me. My mother stepped aside, and I walked in. Seeing her, my heart leapt into my throat. There she was, waiting for me in the traditional mating night garb I always hoped she would wear for me. But, at the moment, she was looking at me horrified.

"Bedding ceremony?" She squeaked.

I stepped forward immediately trying to comfort her, but she screamed and bolted to the other side of the room.

"Sybine," I breathed. I never wanted her afraid of me.

"I cannae do this! I cannae!"

"Sybine," the command in my mother's voice surprised me but it had a calming effect on my mate. Sybine looked over at her and allowed her to approach. "Cahal is alone, Finn and Kai are distracting the rest. There is no reason to be this way. Now, be at ease."

Sybine took a deep breath and nodded slowly. Her eyes drifted to mine and I tried to smile gently but from the way she grimaced, I was sure I looked like a hungry dragon ready to devour her. My mother gently touched my back and headed to the door.

I followed and after she left, I barred the door. Sybine sank down on the side of the bed and wrapped her arms around herself. I desperately needed a distraction of having her in my room. I went to my desk and poured a cup of wine. Much preferring ale or whiskey, wine was the traditional fare for mating nights.

She watched me intently, but I did not look over at her. Instead, I paced to the fire and gazed deeply into my black flame. Sighing, I took a drink. It was not as if I did not know she would be hesitant given our history, but it is not like we had never been together. I knew she would be worried, even nervous but I did not expect sheer terror.

My dragon sulked and again I wondered if I did the right thing. She was afraid of me. How could I condemn her to this life?

"I ken you are scared of me. I ken I have treated you poorly in the past. I ken you must hate that I am the one standing here instead of him. If you so desire, I will petition our mating be reversed. 'Tis no' too late. That way you could have a chance at a better relationship. With someone you have less... history. I would not have you living in fear of me." It broke my heart to say it, but it was the truth. There was no noise from her direction and as I drained the wine with the express purpose of gathering my fortitude to leave and seek out Finn, I felt her heat at my side and her hand on my arm.

Turning to her, I looked deeply in her eyes seeing her dragon peek out.

"I am sorry, Cahal," she said. "I do not want you to reverse our mating. I only ask you to give me time. You know I have always loved you but after everything... I need time and I need to know you still look at me as the female you once loved. I am different, so are you, but I thank you for offering what not many males would offer. I do not want to stop this, but I am scared, not of you of what we meant to each other. Please understand."

I nodded. "I do, lass and have only myself to blame. If I were not so rash, I would have seen it. You believed you were carrying my whelp, did you no'?"

She swallowed and looked away but nodded. "And you were going to be War Chief, you could not marry me. Bearcbhan came upon me crying and when the whole story came out, he offered what you did not."

So my youngest brother was more honorable than me. He would have raised my whelp as his own simply because my mate needed a name.

"But when I found out I was no' carrying, I told him, thinking he would release us. But he told me he loved me and so long as I accepted, we would stay mated."

"You had not..."

She shook her head. "Nay, we had not been together. But by then, you hated me, and I could never do that to either of you. So we stayed mated and had our beautiful whelps. And now, he is gone. Never say I hoped it had been you instead, that is untrue.

I merely wished it had never happened, but I can never say I wish I had never mated because without him, I would not have my family."

I turned to her and took her hands. "Your whelps will always have me. And you will as well. Aye, I was angry, I hated the situation but never you. Can we go ahead from here? Be friends and partners?"

"For now..." she blushed and looked down. "I have always loved you, Cahal."

"I have always loved you," I stated. "Could we agree to start over? My brother deserves to be properly mourned."

She took a deep breath. "He does, but I have missed you so terribly. Can you hold me tonight?"

"Sybine, you ken I would and could never deny you anything, but I do not think it would be wise for my dragon to be that close to you."

"Please?" She begged.

I never could deny her. Nodding, I agreed, though I knew I would get no sleep that night.

Chapter Four

Kai MacKay, War Chief of Clan MacKay

 could not sleep. Thoughts of Tahra raced through my mind. I itched to know my true feelings. I knew I cared for her more than any female of my acquaintance, but I did not know if I could love, let alone give her the love she deserved. Walking up to the battlements, I greeted my men on watch.

"All quiet?" I asked.

"Aye," Drake, my sergeant-at-arms told me.

I rested my hands on the waist height wall, my thumb aching with a phantom pain of the cut that had already healed. I knew my affection for Tahra was known to the family, I had been accepted as her escort on more than one occasion, but to hear Finn say it, made my cheeks ache with the perpetual grin on my face. Though it would have to be her choice. As a princess, I could not request her hand, she would have to speak with me. I could however discuss the idea with her father and brother and tell them of my affections and desires. Fortunately, Tahra and I had discussed it before, and she seemed amenable to the idea.

My dragon preened in the back of my mind as I thought about her. My true mate. The question of my proclivities... the brothers seemed to constantly discuss was not true. Let me amend. What they saw, me looming over one of the human women I frequented in the village pub, my eyes in my dragon form and her wrists tied to the headboard with a piece of silk was not *my* idea. She had a fantasy to be *rescued* by a dragon but taken before the dragon let her go. I know, I shook my head, but, I was all too willing to play the part but it was consensual. It always was. Granted, I had not been back to see her since, but I was perturbed Finn and Cahal could not let it go.

Besides, it was not my choice to fall in love with my best friend's sister, daughter of my king. But it happened. Her laughter was like a sweet song to my heart. Her intelligence, wit, and beauty was the thing I needed more than my next breath.

Breathing in the crisp night air, my cheeks ached again, and I chuckled as I gazed out at the inky blackness. Dark never mattered to dragons as our vision was just as good during the day or night. I was lost in my thoughts when Drake walked up beside me.

"Tell me you want to be alone, and I'll leave," he said. Shaking my head, I greeted him. "What robs your sleep?"

"Nothing," I replied.

"Ah, a female then?"

I was never one to moon over a lass, but never had I known my true mate and have happiness within reach.

"Tell me, Drake," I started. "How did you approach Kiara's father?"

Drake's eyebrows rose, "is that what's on your mind? Has a lass actually turned the head of our fearless War Chief?"

I gave him a side glance. Drake leaned his elbows on the battlements and looked out.

"My only advice, my friend, is do not wait around. You are a strong warrior, you deserve to be happy. If you care for this female, be sure to tell her and do not expect her to just know."

Drake's hand landed on my back in a firm pat as he was called away. I lowered to my elbows on the battlements looking out. My thoughts consumed me but not enough to ignore the movement to my right. Three males moved stealthily among the shadows. But the odd thing was, they were moving away from the keep and one was carrying something over their shoulder. My dragon eyes took over and I zeroed in on the bundle. I had never seen the males before, but there was something about the bundle they carried. When blonde hair peeked out from beneath the cloak thrown over it, my heart stopped.

Tahra.

"Sound the alarm!" I bellowed. Drake ran over to me, but

my dragon took over and I shifted with a roar. Jumping into the air, I beat my massive wings and flew, hearing the alarm rise behind me. Those men just stole the princess, the love of my life. They would be ashes before the night was out.

Cahal

I woke to pounding on my door. Holding Sybine to my side, I blinked sleep away. The pounding increased but they could not enter with the bar in place. Sybine woke with a start and when her sleepy eyes found mine, her brows furrowed, but the pounding continued.

"Cahal!" It was Father. "Open up, we are under attack."

"What?" I breathed. Quickly throwing the bedclothes off us, I made sure Sybine was covered in her thin nightdress before I opened the door. Father's face was ashen. "What has happened?"

"It is your sister. She has been taken."

"Taken?" I demanded. "By whom?"

"We do not know," Da' said. "Kai rose the alarm, he saw it and shifted. Drake is on the battlements with Finn. We must hurry."

"Of course," I answered. Grabbing my plaid and wrapping it around my waist over my tunic. Turning back to my mate in our bed, her face held nothing but terror and yet the underlying strength that I always loved was there. She stood and wrapped her plaid aristad around her.

"I will go to her highness. Where is she?" She spoke of my mother. When the king and queen stepped down, their titles revert to highness.

"She is on the battlements ready to shift and fly after Kai," da' said.

"Let us go," I stated and we hurried to the end of the corridor, then up the stairs leading to the battlements. My eyes caught Finn and my mother speaking to Drake. Though my mother outwardly looked calm, I could see the raging fire in her eyes and pitied the enemy who took her daughter.

"Finn," I called and ran up to him, with Sybine by my side. After a quick bow to show respect, I demanded to know what happened.

"I donnae ken," Finn answered. "I only heard Kai's bellow and ran up here."

"Should I go to her majesty?" Sybine asked.

"If you would, I would not have her alone knowing my wife's desire to join us. I cannae allow her to be taken or injured," Finn said.

"I go now," Sybine replied and after a quick look at me, she touched my arm and left.

"Tell me quickly, Drake," I said.

"All I ken, my lord, is, Kai was up here, we were speaking and then I heard him yell. I raced to where he stood and saw three men all cloaked, carrying something over their shoulder. It was a figure with blonde hair. When he shifted, I raised the alarm."

"Did you see the figure? Was it my sister?" Finn demanded.

"It must be," Drake replied. "No other would cause Kai to react like that."

"I checked in on her," Mother started. "She is not in her room and her companion was drugged by Dragon Bane."

I snarled. "How did they get past our defenses?"

"We will discuss that later," Finn answered. "Now, we must go and save our sister."

"I fly with you, my king," Drake stated. "I ken the direction they were going."

"Were they dragon?" Da' asked.

"I ken no', majesty," Drake replied.

"Bastards," Finn muttered. "We waste time, let us go."

Chapter Five

Tahra

Slowly, I came to feeling a horrible ache in my stomach. With every bounce, something jabbed into my ribs. Opening my eyes, it was an odd sensation to see upside down. Only then did I realize I was being carried over someone's shoulder. Suddenly remembering what happened, I screeched but felt the chains around my wrists. The man, who's shoulder I was currently slung over like a sack of potatoes, smacked my arse with a stinging slap.

"Say nothing and don't think about moving about," he hissed.

I didn't have long to say or do anything.

Unceremoniously stolen from my room, thrown over a very smelly male's shoulder and impudently dropped to the hard wooden planks of a galley ship, my dignity hardly recovered. Standing as well as I could after having woken in chains, unable to shift and defend myself unless I wanted broken wrists and ankles, I looked around me.

"I demand to know what is going on. Do you have any idea who I am?"

"That's the whole idea, princess." The way the smelly male spat my title sounded more like an insult. "Cast off," he shouted to the men around us. "Let's get this trip started. I'd still like to be young when we get to Ireland."

"Ireland?" I questioned more to myself.

"Young?" One of the other sailors, or rather disgusting pirates, shouted back. "Aye, you just want to wenches to port, Arnol."

The man before me, Arnol, made a crude gesture by grabbing the front of his trousers.

"What do you want with me?" I demanded feeling the boat rock as we pushed off the dock. The man did not reply. "I asked you a question, Pirate. I demand an answer. What do you want with me? Where are we going?"

The man and crew laughed.

"Well, what I *want* with you is too crass for a *lady,*" he again made the crude gesture. "But Korlon won't pay if the goods are damaged. Still, it wouldn't be too much to have a little fun, eh lads? I'd like to show you what happens when wenches use that smart mouth against me. Ole Arnol doesn't take too kindly to a demanding woman. Should put you in your place, I should."

"I know my place. And it's far superior to the smelly likes of you." He took a menacing step toward me. "Be careful," I went on. "I am a dragon shifter. Even in human form, I can still blow a little fire. Enough to burn you and your ship."

He seemed to think better about it and stepped back. His eyes grew wide as he looked over my head. Then, I heard it. A roar. I whipped around. It was a dragon.

In the darkness, I could not see who it was but the iridescent blue flame expelled from his mouth told me who it was. "Kai," I breathed.

Smelly Arnol grabbed me from behind and held me tightly.

"Row boys! It won't hurt us with her on board!"

The boat lurched as the crew jumped to the oars.

"Kai!" I screamed. The dragon's head whipped around to see me. Smoke curled out of his nose.

"This your woman?" Arnol shouted up to him. "The only way for her to live, is if you let us go. Don't worry. We'll take good care of her." I felt something hot and slimy caress my ear. The stench was overpowering, and it took everything in me not to lose my dinner all over the planks.

Arnol tugged me to the other side of the boat, the door to the belly of the ship before us. I fought against his hold stepping back hard on his foot, breaking every bone. I used what strength I had, which was more than the average human woman.

Forcing my head back, I made contact with his nose. I saw stars for a moment but heard the crack of his bone. He cursed words I hadn't ever heard before and threw me down on piles of what felt like grain bags.

"I'll teach you to fight me," he spat, blood from his broken nose dripping as he dropped to his knees and slid over me. I screamed and fought. Remembering Brigid always had me keep a knife in my sock, since her father, a War Chief, had shown her how to fight in small spaces, I allowed Arnol to pull up my skirts just enough for me to grab it. I refused to allow him anymore. Kai bellowed above me and let out his blue flame. I heard screams of the crew and the roar of fire as it consumed flesh, bone, and wooden hull.

Arnol looked up from where he had buried his head into my chest. It was all I needed. Slashing with the cool steel it quickly turned hot as his blood gushed over it. Grabbing the keys from his belt, I lifted my knee hard and struck him where Cahal taught me to strike a male if I was ever in danger. Arnol gurgled as he grabbed his slit throat but as the light faded in his eyes, he slumped forward dead. Shoving him off me, I unlocked my fetters that held my ankles, I had just gotten both wrists free when Kai circled around again.

Without thought, I raced to the edge of the burning boat and jumped into the water ducking my head below the surface as Kai burned even more. Once the fire died above me, I came up out of the water and shifted. My dragon kicked to shore.

Out of the water, I took flight, soaring into the sky. I found Kai coming around for a third time. He saw me and roared again. I called back, letting him know I was fine then clenched my front talon. I wanted to be the one to sink the boat. Kai nodded once. I coasted on the wind.

Taking a deep breath, I relished the burning acid in my throat and blew it out directly on to the body of my smelly captor. When next I looked, he was a pile of ash and many of the crew were either dead or floundering in the water. Kai called to me and motioned the other way. I nodded and he came beside me, his wing touching mine in a dragon embrace. We flew toward home. Knowing at the moment, I was experiencing a rush of adrenaline, I fully expected the terror of my experiences that evening to wash over me once I was safe. Though, flying next to Kai, I never felt safer.

Cahal

Finn, Da', Mum, Drake, and I, along with fifty other dragon warriors, flew as fast as we could in the direction Drake had seen Kai fly. Praying for the first time in a long time, I hoped Kai found my sister, and if she was unable to save herself, saved her from whatever horrid plans the jackanape bastards had in store for her. The thought made me sick. Glancing over at my mother, her majestic white dragon glided gracefully but the power in her movements and the set of her jaw made me proud, and sorry for the blackguard who stole Tahra. Finn flew at the head of the V, Drake and myself at his sides. The darkness was just to that point where humans claimed it was the darkest but suddenly before us about two leagues ahead of us, we saw hot blue flames explode into the night sky. Finn pulled up and we all coasted until we could assess what was happening.

Recognizing Kai's flame, my heart slowed a little. He found her. Our pause only lasted a moment and as soon as Finn gave a soft roar, we continued. More fire lit the night sky, then a second color joined the blue. Tahra's purple. Again, Finn slowed, assessing.

It did not take long for us to see the two dragons flying toward us. One blue and the other a light lavender. Our sister was safe. I felt the rush of relief we all must have felt.

Finn called to them and Kai gave a short roar back, then when they were close enough, bowed his head to him. Finn motioned for the fifty dragons to surround both Tahra and our mother who had gone to greet our sister and check to make sure she was well.

Kai growled when Drake took his position beside Tahra. Finn looked toward them and nodded, giving Drake a different assignment. I caught my brother's eye and if dragons could roll their pupils he would have. I chortled and wished dragons could communicate in their forms, I had a few choice things to remind him about. Finn was just as bad with his mate.

Instead, Finn turned and as a unit protecting our princess, we flew home.

Chapter Six

Tahra

We flew home, Kai at my side and my brother's guards encompassing Mama and me. When I saw Kai coming to my aid, I fell deeper in love with him. Seeing that odious man over my trying to hurt me and trying to take what did not belong to him, made me want Kai all the more. The horror of what I went through slowly came over me and as home came into view,

I was shaking.

Fortunately, if anyone saw, they did nothing. The males waited until Mama and I landed on the queen's ledge. Brigid and Sybine waited for us. Kai landed beside me but Finn gnashed his teeth. Males were not permitted to watch the females shift. Not only was seeing the female form nude after a shift embarrassing to us, the dragon males were highly physical and only mated couples were allowed to shift together and only when they were alone. Kai growled back but I yipped, and he looked at me. I nodded, telling him I was all right. Kai huffed but agreed and jumped off the ledge landing far below in the bailey. Da', Finn, and Cahal waited until the rest of his males had landed to leave us.

Mama and I shifted quickly and accepted the shifts from Brigid and Sybine. Once covered, Mama took me tightly in her arms, holding me close.

"Are you all right, love?" she asked.

"Aye, Mama. The male tried to... he tried..." I couldn't continue as my body shook so desperately.

"Oh, shh, shh," she held me closer. "But he didn't and how he's dust." She cupped my face and kissed my forehead. "You're safe."

I nodded but my body still shook. Mama looked over at my sisters-by-mating. "Do you have any whiskey?" she asked.

"Finn does," Brigid said, and we followed her into the king's suite. Mama and Da' had moved down the hall allowing Finn and Brigid, now king and queen, to have the quarters. It was odd for me not to see Mama's things, but it was a needed tradition.

Brigid pressed a cup into my hand. The pungent alcohol

burned my nostrils. Mama coaxed me to take a large sip. Grimacing, as I drank, the affects were warming and calming. Soon, the shaking stopped and my three female family members embraced me. I was safe.

Eventually, my mother pushed my hair out of my face and smiled softly at me. "We need to go to Finn. He needs to know what happened, love. And I am sure Kai needs to see you to make sure you're well."

I nodded and Brigid went to the chest near the hearth. Pulling out two plaid *aristads*, we both covered ourselves further and all four of us went to Finn's solar.

Cahal

The males said nothing as we shifted quickly and dressed in our plaids. The warriors took up their posts and the rest of us headed up to Finn's solar. We waited for the females to arrive as Kai paced before the door, his agitation felt by all.

"Anything I need to know before my sister arrives, Kai?" Finn asked.

Kai looked over at him, his eyes flashing between his human and dragon slits. "Aye, the bastard tried to force himself on her. She fought him off. He's dust."

Our brows rose. Though he did not directly say Tahra killed the male, it was inferred from Kai's anger.

"Finn," he finally sighed, his eyes back to human. "I am sorry. I should have protected her better. I should never have allowed anyone to touch her. The keep was not secure. I am uncertain how that happened but if you let me, I will discover it. I will accept whatever punishment you decree. But please, let me redeem myself and discover who is responsible."

"Punishment?" Finn questioned.

"Aye," he lowered his head. "I should have made sure the keep was secured. They should not have been able to get in and hurt her."

"The keep is as secure as it always is, Kai. This is not your fault. In fact, had you not raised the alarm, my sister may have been violated, stolen away, and never seen again. Your heroism is to be praised not punished."

Finn walked over to him and offered his arm in a warrior's shake. Kai gazed up at him and accepted the offer.

"You have proven yourself time and time again that you are the best choice for my sister's mate. Should you seek to pursue her, I will accept your request with my blessing and happiness."

Kai's face lifted as his chest heaved a sigh. "Thank you," he gushed. "I love your sister, my king. I did not know my feelings, I'll be honest. But the thought of losing her and the possibility of it tonight, has made me understand them all the more. I do wish it. But I must speak with her first."

"Admirably done," Finn smiled and looked over at Da' who nodded and then to me. I hadn't seen much of Kai's relationship with my sister, but he was an honorable male and as such, deserving of the princess. I agreed with my brother but before more could be said, there was a knock at the door and Brigid's scent filled the room as she peered in.

"We are ready, Finn," she said.

Out of respect for her and her title, we all bowed.

"Come in, love," Finn reached for her and she took his

hand. Following in behind her was Mum, Tahra, and... my mate, Sybine. Furtive glances my way, she smiled slightly, and I bowed to her.

Happy with my dragon's silence, it was hard to believe we were mated that same day. So much had happened.

Tahra went to our father and embraced him then to Finn and me. Finally, she reached Kai.

"Thank you," she said softly. "If you had not come when you did..."

"You would have found a way, princess," he said. "You are strong. I am just so glad I was able to reach you before anything worse happened."

She nodded but I still saw the shakiness in her shoulders.

"We won't keep you long, love," Finn stepped forward. "I just need to know anything and everything you saw or heard. We need to find out who if anyone sent those males to abduct you."

"I'll tell you what I remember," she agreed but did not move from Kai's side. After a moment to gather her thoughts, she began. "I heard a noise in my chamber and woke to find Fenora lying on the floor away from her palette. Immediately, I got up to check on her and that's when I heard someone in the shadows. A male grabbed me from behind and before I had a chance to fight or even breathe, they knocked me unconscious. When I woke, they had placed chains on my wrists. I could not shift without fear of breaking bones and I knew I would need my strength to escape. I was slung over the male's shoulder and my ankles were secured by more fetters. I could not call out and when I came too, I moved and tried to scream but the male..."

smacked my backside. I kept quiet after that." She looked down and we all waited. "How is Fenora?" she asked suddenly.

"She's resting. They gave her Dragon Bane," Brigid explained. "I have checked on her and Duncan is with her now."

The young healer in training under his mother was indispensable several months ago when Finn was injured with the same sickening toxin.

"Oh good, thank you, Brigid," she said. "They kept a hood over my head until we reached the boat. When I was finally able to see, I noticed there were about ten males all doing various tasks. I found out the male who abducted me, was the leader and his name was Arnol. He ordered the males to get a move on. Something about Ireland and ports... also there was mention of wenches and certain things Arnol liked to do." Her cheeks flamed and she looked away. Kai wrapped his arm around her shoulders, and she leaned into him. "I demanded to know what they wanted with me. They said what they *want* isn't the issue. But he also said there were *other* things he would do to me. Korlon wouldn't pay if the goods were damaged. I warned him that I was a dragon shifter, but he didn't seem too off put by that fact. He..." she trailed off.

"It's all right, love," our mother stepped forward. "You're safe now."

She nodded. "He threw me down and came on top of me. He tried to... touch me. Kai had just arrived and Arnol ordered the males to row saying Kai wouldn't hurt them if they kept me close."

"He yelled something up to me and I saw him lick her ear," Kai said. Tahra shuddered and touched the mentioned flesh. "It boiled my blood. I saw him grab Tahra and take her to the back of the boat. That was when I blew out my fire."

"And thank the gods he did. I was able to get the knife from my sock and cut his throat then got the keys to my fetters off Arnol's belt. When my chains gave way, I jumped off the boat and into the water. My dragon pushed forward and we shifted, flying up to Kai's side. Arnol was dead."

"Good," Da' grunted.

"Once he was killed and the boat clearly destroyed, we flew together. You know what happened after that," Kai finished.

"Were all crew members dead?" Finn asked.

"Some were in the water, my king. My one thought was to get her highness home to safety."

Finn nodded slowly then turned to me. "Send some dragons back to the site and make sure only one survives. I want to talk to that one."

I bowed to him but saw Kai's reaction. As War Chief, he should have been the one to carry out the king's orders. Finn must have seen it too because he continued.

"Kai, go with my sister. I place her under your protection. Do whatever you must to keep her safe, no fear of reprisals. If that means being in her room unchaperoned, I trust you both. I caution you, but I trust you. Allow what we discussed earlier to happen first."

I thought back. Finn wanted Kai and Tahra mated before they were physically intimate and in Tahra's current vulnerable and emotional state, he warned him not to take it too far. Then, he looked back at me.

"I am sorry to ask this of you on your mating night, Cahal, but—"

"Fear not, my king. It will be done. My mate understands." I looked back at Sybine. She nodded and in that moment, I missed her and what we were to each other.

"Good," Finn walked to our sister and kissed her forehead. "'Tis glad I am you are safe, sister. I am sorry it happened in the first place, but glad Kai saw you and was able to help get you home. You are so strong. Let yourself go through the fear now, aye?"

She nodded and hugged him.

"Now," Finn pulled back. "I need to council with Da' and Cahal. Kai, go with my sister. That is your charge."

"Aye, my king." Kai and our females left the room. Sybine turned to look at me before she left. I nodded to her and the corner of her lip tipped up. I could not wait to return to our room and hold her to me again.

After speaking to some of my warriors, I watched as they took to the sky to return to the dock to see if any humans who attacked Tahra lived. The gleam in their eye told me they would be happy to defend the honor of the princess. Once my task was done, I hurried back inside to da's... *Finn's* solar.

Finding Finn and Da' sitting in the chairs with a glass of whisky in their hands, I paused. It was a usual image but odd now that Finn was king.

"All well?"

"Aye, my males will be back shortly."

"Good."

I watched him as he went to the side table and poured

another cup of whisky. Passing it to me, we all drank in silence allowing Finn to think. When he huffed a sigh and sat back into his chair, he looked up at us both and motioned to the other chair.

"Please, don't make me offer you a seat when we're alone. We are family first," he said.

"Understood," I answered and saw.

"This is not exactly how I expected my first day of being king would go. It hasn't even been a full day."

"Aye," Da' replied. "But you did well, Finn. Better, even."

"I could have lost our sister," Finn rebutted.

"You gave Kai the responsibility to watch her. Knowing his love for her, he is the best choice," I replied.

"So I exploited his feelings?"

"Nay," Da' answered. "You used the best at your disposal."

Finn nodded and I saw some of the worry behind his green eyes dissipate. Leaning forward, he looked at both of us.

"I cannae ignore the fact Tahra mentioned Ireland as their destination. Do either of you know the male she mentioned? Korlon?"

I shook my head. I had never heard the name before. Looking over at Da', I caught his negative response.

"There must be a connection. Who in Ireland would want Tahra?" He asked.

"She and your mother have visited your uncles many times without me. I donnae ken, son," Da' said. "But we could find out."

Finn nodded slowly. "Do you think Uncle Rexian had anything to do with this?"

It was on the tip of my tongue to defend the uncle with whom I fostered. Five years of my adolescence I spent over in Ireland under the dragon king, my grandfather. He was a horrible leader, and the clan hated him but Uncle Rexian, the eldest of seven sons, mated and had sons of his own when I was there. Many years' age difference between my cousins and me, they were still merely boys though they were in their late teens in dragon years. Uncle Rexian and Uncle Raeghar; the second eldest, were the greatest warriors in the clan, and they taught me. Raeghar was the first to tell me to try for War Chief. The first to believe in me.

"I think it would be a good idea to go speak with your uncle," Da' said.

"Indeed," Finn agreed. "Cahal, I again hate to have to ask, but would you come with us? Of any of us, Uncle Rexian is most likely to listen to you."

"Of course," I answered.

"You misunderstand me, lad," Da' started. "*I* will not be joining you. Perhaps Drake?"

"Why? Da', I need you."

Da' shook his head. "Nay, they need to see you as king. I will only complicate the issue."

Finn stared at our father for a long moment, then eventually nodded.

"We leave after dawn. Get some rest." Finn stood and took a deep breath.

"Name someone to be in charge while you're away, lad,"

Da' offered.

"You, of course."

Again, Da' shook his head. "I am honored but it would be best for clan unity if I stay stepped down."

"Then Kai," he sighed.

"Good," Da' agreed. "You'll get your head above water, lad. You'll see. I am very proud of you."

Having heard those words from da' recently, I knew the affect it had on a son. Finn puffed out his chest a little and dipped his head in thanks.

Then, looking at me, he spoke low. "We leave for Uncle Rexian's kingdom tomorrow without stops. I need to speak with Drake then if the males have returned with the prisoner, will you join me in questioning him?"

"Aye."

"Good, I will seek my bed after, be sure to have them wake me if I am asleep."

"I will," I swore and followed da' out of the king's solar, hearing Finn call for the guard who stood outside to bring Drake to him as a matter of urgency.

Chapter Seven

It had been years since I had travelled anywhere past my usual hunting grounds in the highlands north of our island, but as I walked back to my room to prepare for the long journey, I took a deep breath. I loved my uncle as a friend, mentor, and even as a father figure. I prayed he had nothing to do with Tahra's abduction. I didn't think our family could handle any other betrayal from blood. There was nothing worse.

Without thinking, I opened the door of my room and froze as Sybine's bare form greeted my eyes. Her back was to me as she poured more steaming water into the copper tub. Her smooth, clear skin beckoned to me and my hands ached to touch. Even my dragon was stunned and simply stared.

Suddenly, clearly hearing the door, Sybine gasped and whirled around... Stunning. Shamefully, I stared taking in the changes to her body since the last time I saw her like that. Her breasts were larger, filled with the milk for her young, her stomach was not as flat nor as taut but the marks she bore were beautiful. They were the scars of bringing three wonderful whelps into the world. Her hips were wider, flared for better delivery and nothing looked more beautiful to me.

My perusal happened in mere moments as she grasped the plaid nearest her and covered her nude form, but though it was only seconds, it felt like hours. As soon as the tantalizing changes were covered, guilt flared in my belly. I turned away and cleared my throat.

"Forgive me. I should have knocked."

She said nothing for a moment, my dragon sensing fear and shame.

"'Tis all right," she finally answered, her voice rough. "I was not expecting you so soon. I hope it is agreeable to utilize your bath."

"Of course," I replied, wanting to turn and assure her but keeping my eyes firmly fixed away. "My apologies. I will not be so careless again."

"'Tis all right, Cahal. I am your mate. This is your room. I am the one who should apologize."

"There is no need," I answered. My heart thumped when she said the word *mate*. "And this is *our* room. I would leave you to your bath, but I must pack."

"Pack?" her voice questioned and I could see the quirk of her brows even in my mind.

"Finn and I leave tomorrow morning for Ireland."

"Ireland?" She asked.

"Aye."

"Please turn, I am covered," she said.

Taking a deep breath, I did as she asked and saw she was covered in a thin chemise and the plaid over her shoulders. We looked at each other for some time before she spoke.

"Why are you going to Ireland?"

"With what Tahra said, Finn thinks it best to speak with our Uncle Rexian."

"You fostered with him, did you not?"

"Aye," my chest swelled with surprise that she remembered. "Technically, with our grandfather as he was king, but Uncle Rexian was..."

"Your favorite?" she questioned.

"Aye, he was indeed."

"I remember you speaking fondly of him."

"He is a good friend. Like a second father to me. Finn and I leave just after dawn."

"Allow me to pack for you. 'Tis my duty."

I stared at her. It was a mate's duty, if she so desired, to pack her male's things. It was not meant to lower a female, rather males realized after many years of forgetting or missing something when they packed, their mates usually remembered and packed extra than what was needed. Many times I remembered my father was surprised by a *cèilidh* and worried he did not have the appropriate attire, only to know my mother had thought of it and packed his best tunic and plaid.

Sybine did not wait for my answer, instead, she moved to the chest at the foot of my bed and opened it. My eyes followed her every movement, then drifted back to the steaming bath.

"Your water will get cold. This can keep and I do not mind packing myself." I had done it every trip for fifteen years. Though I was twenty-seven, I had a servant to assist me when I was younger.

Sybine stopped and looked over at me, guilt washed over her face. "Forgive me," she moved away from the chest. "Of course, since we are not proper mates, you donnae wish for my assistance."

"What do you mean *proper* mates?" I questioned.

"I mean," she looked away, then glanced at the bed. The meaning was clear as day.

"You mean, since we have nae consummated our mating?" I offered. She nodded. Walking over to her, I spoke low. "We have been together many times before, Sybine." I watched as her cheeks pinked. "That is not the reason. I simply did not want you to wait on me while your bath is cooling. Please know, I do not need to make love to you to view you as my mate. In my eyes, and that of my dragon, we are one."

She stared at me, searching my face. Her dragon was sitting watching me. I wanted nothing more than to pull her into me and kiss her, but I could not. Not yet.

"Thank you for wanting to pack for me. But please go and enjoy your bath. I will keep my eyes averted."

She looked away, cheeks again going pink. "I hope," she began, then cleared her throat. "I hope you did not abhor what you saw. After three whelps, a female's body changes drastically. I know I am not the same as I once was; what, perhaps, you remember me being."

I stared at her. The memory of her from before had faded the instant I saw her that night. I did not want what she was previously, I wanted her now. Taking a silent breath, I shook my head and swallowed. "Nay, nothing abhorrent, Sybine."

She took a shaky breath and forced a smile. Turning from me, I instantly felt the absence of her heat. I closed my eyes, attempting to calm my racing heart and desire for her. Though it had been five years since we had been together, a betrayal, death, and pain culminating in those years, my body still reacted to her as it had always done. Not wanting to look away as she slowly slipped the chemise off one shoulder, glancing at me, I clenched my fists and turned. Out of respect for her and my late brother, I stalked to my chest and strained not to listen to the rustle of clothes and the soft splash of water as she stepped into the tub but both sounds rattled in my ears louder than a dragon's roar and I grit my teeth. Staying away from her was harder than I thought it would be. Perhaps it was a good thing I was going with Finn to Ireland. I needed to get away from Sybine. I couldn't trust myself.

"Cahal," she called and every part of me froze, even the breath in my chest. "Could you open the balcony doors? It is grown over warm with your fire."

It took me a moment to process her request then,

turning with my back still toward her, I shuffled my way to the two doors leading to my balcony. Once they were open and the crisp evening air permeated around me, I filled my lungs to capacity and held my breath. The air cooled my heated skin and cleared the cobwebs of my mind. Part of me wanted to go back into the room, scoop her up out of the bath, lay her on my bed, and make love to her the way I always thought I would on our mating night. But the other, knew she would never want me to and would run from me screaming. I would never force her, never make her regret. Letting my breath out slowly, I listened.

The water sloshed as she must have washed her hair. The beautiful blonde locks. I ached to wrap my fingers around them. Setting my hands on the balustrade, I tried to clear my mind for the task at hand. The extra patrol Finn had ordered, marched below me and on the battlements above. Some dragons flew high in the sky watching.

I looked down when I heard a commotion. Looking down, I saw the patrol I had sent to capture the remaining men who had hurt my sister return. Wishing I had been able to join them, as my dragon itch to fly, my first duty was to Finn, the clan, then Sybine.

Sensing Sybine behind me, it did not surprise me when her voice rang out, "What is happening?"

"The males returned with one of the humans who took Tahra. Finn will be questioning him soon," I explained.

"But he must rest," she walked out onto the balcony and stood beside me, looking down at the man in chains, then up at me. "The king will be too tired if he does not rest for the journey."

"It is not over long," I justified. "We will be fine."

"We?"

"Aye," I replied. "As soon as I can finish my packing, I will join Finn in questioning the man below and then, we fly to Ireland."

"Then let me finish for you and you go to the king," she offered.

It was the best option. "Aye, thank you, Sybine."

"Of course," she answered, her eyes bright and her skin flushed with the heat of the water from her bath. "If there is anything else I can do, let me know."

I could not stop my fingers, they moved of their own volition and gently stroked her cheek. She did not flinch away, and her lips tipped up. Lowering my hand, I bowed my head toward her.

"I should go. Finn will need me."

As soon as I rose my head out of a bow, her hands came on either side of my face and she rammed her lips onto mine. I floundered, caught off guard. Before I could return her kiss, she pulled away and heaved a sigh.

"I needed to do that," she said. "I am sorry for attacking you as I did, but I found I was desperate to feel your kiss before you leave."

By then, I had my wits about me and took her hand in mine. "I would be honored to kiss you properly."

She debated as she always did, her one eyelid lower than the other and her teeth biting the inside of her cheek. When she hadn't answered in the appropriate time, I dropped the idea and stepped back, my waist bumping the stone balustrade.

"I must go," I said, then moved past her.

"Cahal," she called as soon as I had reentered the bedroom. Turning, we locked eyes and I watched as determination entered her crystal blue depths. I let it be her decision. I could not decide for her, but as soon as she took one step then another, my dragon sat up in the back of my mind. He roared but I tamped him down.

Behave. I ordered with as much dominance as I could muster. My dragon settled just in time.

Sybine stood before me, her eyes flashing between dragon slits and human round. Slowly, she raised her hands and placed them on my forearms. My skin burned everywhere she touched as she slid them up my forearms to my upper arms then onto my shoulders eventually stopping with her hands tangled in my hair. She tugged slightly and I lowered my lips to hers.

I felt the soft tingle of her breath on my chin as she closed her eyes. I could wait no longer. Closing the distance between us, I pressed my mouth against hers. Her movements were tentative at first but soon she emboldened and as my tongue slid across the seam of her lips, she opened to me. Her flavor exploded in my mouth, a little wine, something sweet like honey, and all Sybine.

There were nights I would lay awake while on patrol and crave her taste. She was addictive and for five long years... I hated it every time I had to watch Bearcbhan kiss her, knowing what it felt like, tasted like, and how much I missed it.

She whimpered and pulled closer to me. Her body lined with mine. I could feel the changes in her and I loved every one of them. I wanted to explore. I needed to see all her changes. The kiss was not nearly enough. *Perhaps,* I thought. With a gentle nudge, I lifted her into my arms. Our lips never separated as she wrapped her legs around my waist. With quick steps, I reached the bed, my knees hitting it before my mind comprehended. We both landed with a bounce though our lips never parted.

Knowing my weight would be too much for her, I pulled up and rested on my elbows. My lips and tongue still played with hers. Her nails moved to my back and she tore at my tunic pulling it up. Neither of us wanted to break apart even for the moment it would have taken to pull my tunic off.

Her hot little hands pressed against my lower back and I shuddered. It had been years without her, and though I utilized the human pub nearby for those sorts of needs, I had not been back since Nameless' betrayal. I needed her, wanted her, was willing to beg her as she lifted her legs to lock around my waist.

Breaking the kiss, I moved to the place where her jaw, ear, and neck met. It was a sensitive area and I wanted to hear her. She moaned as I sucked on that spot and took my hand placing it on her chest. She always was vociferous, one of the things I loved about her.

But then, like a bucket of water from the icy loch was tossed over me, she moaned; "Bear."

And I froze. I was not my brother.

She had gone still the second she said the name and as I pulled away to look down at her, she would not meet my gaze. It wasn't as if I did nae know she made love to my brother, they had whelps together and the walls were not as thick as Bearcbhan thought they were, but to hear her sigh his name as she was in my arms burned and crushed me.

Getting to my feet as quickly as possible without hurting her, I pulled my tunic down and tucked it into my plaid. Sybine closed her eyes, her body limp.

"I must go," I ground out. I was not angry nor upset with

her. But I could not stay. I needed to cool and be alone. My natural state when I was wounded was to revert to anger or a harsh tone. Even a warrior could be hurt, and I was aching. She opened her eyes and leaned up on her elbows. I could see the effect of our bruising kisses on her red swollen lips and the sadness of an apology in her eyes, but I said nothing.

"Cahal, I—" she began.

"I need to leave," I cut her off. "Finn will be needing me. I will... Be sleeping elsewhere tonight." I could not bring myself to sleep beside her, nor in the same room. My dragon wanted to sulk and lick his invisible wound alone.

Sybine knew us both well-enough to know not to argue. She simply nodded and looked away.

Needing the rush of cold air in my lungs and beneath my wings to heal, I walked to the balcony and with a heaved sigh, I climbed over the balustrade and jumped, shifting into my dragon form as I fell. It felt good to be in dragon form flying high in the night sky. I let the burn of the cold air wipe away the hurt and self-pity. Of course, I did not blame her, there was no one to blame. It simply happened. I wanted her and she needed to feel loved. The fact she spoke her dead husband's name should mean nothing. But it meant everything. Again, I questioned if I had done the right thing.

Chapter Eight

Sybine

My cheeks burned with mortification as I watched Cahal shift and fly. His black dragon was so different from Bearcbhan's golden one but in a way, more beautiful. I looked down at the black Onyx ring on my finger, Cahal's claim. It was a foolish thing to call him back when he walked into the room from the balcony earlier. Foolish and selfish. I missed my husband, his laugh, his touch, the way he could make me feel, and I missed Cahal. But that did not excuse my behavior. I had thrown myself at him and when he questioned, I agreed. Then... again, mortification burned my cheeks. The feel of him pressing me down onto the bed, the heat of his kisses, the need coursing through me, it was shameful. Had I not said Bearcbhan's name, I would not have stopped and we both would have regretted it, now only I regretted it. I hurt him. The big, strong warrior, Cahal was hurt, and it was all my fault. I knew he was not returning that evening even before he spoke. He would not want to be near me.

I lay on his bed long after he left and curled my legs up to be as small as I could. My whelps would be awake soon. They always rose with the dawn just like their father. My eyes filled with tears as I thought about him. His smile, his infectious laugh, his fierce loyalty to the king, the clan, and his family. His love for me and our whelps. How he used to carry Adair on his shoulders as Brogan held his leg. How he reverently rocked Elowyn to sleep every night after I fed her. My heart ached as I sobbed. My daughter would never know, nor remember her father.

Looking over through my tears, I stared at the chair by the fire. We had a similar one in our room, but I closed my eyes remembering. Bearcbhan sitting in his chair before the fire, rocking Elowyn, humming whatever nonsense filled his mind. Our princess long since asleep, but he still stared down at her as if she was the most precious thing in the world, her hand wrapped around his finger, holding tight. I remembered watching from the bed, or the other chair, or even the bath. When he looked over at me, his smile stole my breath. His light golden hair was still dark at its base like it was kissed by the sun. It curled around his head in short cuts, so unlike his two directly eldest brothers; Teyrnon and Cahal. Only Finn had his hair short like Bearcbhan's. His gray eyes, so open, honest, and beautiful stared at me with love, hope, and some heat but holding his daughter, he tempered his reaction to me. The light scruff on his jaw framed perfectly formed lips. His lips were fuller than Cahal's and impossibly smooth. His face was young and handsome with hardly a blemish. I sobbed again. Would his image fade in my mind overtime?

Slowly, he would stand and whisper; "I'll take her to the nursery." I would nod and watch him leave, his powerful back like a shield keeping Elowyn safe. Though the shortest of all his brothers, he still towered over me.

Usually, we kept our daughter with us, but it was his way of asking to make love to me. While he was gone, I pulled down the bedclothes, let a candle or two and splashed rose water on my neck and arms, it was his favorite.

I waited for him to return, eager to love my mate and when he did we loved each other many times. Just before the darkest of the night, Bearcbhan held me close, kissed my hair and told me how much he loved me and how happy I made him. I drifted to sleep hearing his voice naming all the things he was thankful for and blessed by. I would wake at dawn feeling him leave our bed.

"Shh," he would whisper, lean over the bed, and kiss my forehead. "It is not yet time for you to rise, my love. Rest. I'll see to our sons." Every morning he would entertain our boys and ask the nursemaid to feed our daughter so I could sleep and prepare for the day. He was the greatest mate I could have asked for and now he was gone, murdered. My heart broke all over again. All I wanted was to feel his arms around me again holding onto me. My tears refused to stop, and my sobs turned into wails. I knew I would make myself sick, but I could not stop. The door rattled and someone knocked but I could not get up. My body ached from the grief, but I still could not stop. Then, someone grabbed me, someone held me, someone... I looked up to see who was holding me. Cahal. His eyes crazed with concern constantly flashing between dragon and human. I saw his dragon pacing behind his eyes and it only made me cry harder. I never saw Bearcbhan's dragon behind his eyes. He was not my true mate. Cahal was.

Cahal

I flew for only a short time to clear my head and soon stood beside my brother in our dungeons looking at the sniveling male before us. The stench of urine and feces wafting from him, turned my stomach. He wept too, the milksop.

"Why did you steal the Princess this evening?" Finn demanded again. The male cowered and shook with fear.

I stood behind my king, support if he needed it. I knew he did not, but sometimes it was all about perception and at that moment, the coward saw two large dragonmen looming over him. That satisfied a deep dark part of me.

"Answer me," Finn demanded. "And use caution when you speak. I am in no mood for lies nor stuttered truth."

The male looked at Finn and the stench of urine grew. "N-none of us kn-knew the whole plan," he began.

At least he can speak, my dragon said in the back of my mind. My lips turned up as I saw the male react to my eyes flashing to slits as my dragon spoke to me.

"Then tell me what you know," Finn continued.

"Don't kill me!"

"I'll consider it," Finn replied.

"Arnol knew the whole thing. He and Korlon spoke."

"Who or what is Korlon and why did he want the Princess?" Finn questioned.

"I-I don't know!"

Finn shrugged. "Then you are of no further use to me."

I nodded to the guard, and a male to the human's right, grabbed him.

"Wait! Please! I do know something or rather I overheard."

Finn held up a hand to the guard stopping him. "And what did you overhear?"

"Don't kill me!"

"You dare give my king orders?" My dragon bellowed.

A sick sort of satisfaction grew in the pit of my stomach when I saw the man grow deathly pale and tremble. I hadn't been that sort of male for many years.

Easy, I cautioned my dragon. *He does no good to Finn dead.*

He should mind his tongue or I'll burn it out.

You aren't that bloodthirsty dragon anymore.

Aye, well maybe I am when my pride is injured.

Ah, I realized. It was my dragon's way of dealing with our mate's reaction to us. Fortunately, Finn did not question my dragon's outburst.

"Speak. What did you overhear?" I enjoyed seeing the power Finn exuded. He truly was my king and I was so very proud to call him my brother too.

"Arnol was speaking to Dougal, another of our men and one of the ones who helped steal the Princess. Dougal was questioning why and Arnol said Korlon made a deal with the Irish dragon king for the princess' hand, and we were to take her to him."

I felt a figurative punch to my gut. Our Uncle Rexian was the last dragon king in Ireland. The other clans had died out due to the lack of female dragons. If Korlon had made a deal with the Irish dragon king...

Finn looked at me and I motioned my head to the door behind us. I could not let the male see how his words stole my breath.

Finn walked out of the dungeon cell but stopped when he heard the male beg for his life once more. Turning, Finn looked past me, and then to the guard.

"Keep him here, alive, for now, while I investigate his claim."

The guard bowed and the male sobbed.

Finn and I walked together, leaving the foul stench of decay and excrement and into the clean crisp Highland night air.

Filling our lungs and cleansing our senses, Finn looked at me. "That was a damning statement," he said.

"I cannae believe it. I could more believed Da' conspired. Uncle Rexian loves Tahra I cannae believe it, Finn. I donnae believe it."

"Then what do you make of what he said?" Finn's tone was calm, not accusatory which helped my nerves.

"Saving his own scales," I answered. Even though I

kenned humans had nae scales, it was a common enough phrase for dragons.

"We need to be sure if Uncle Rexian did do this," Finn held up his hand stopping me from speaking. "I donnae want to believe it any more than you do. But if he did, we must know why and for certain. I cannot have a war."

"It seems the best way to prevent it from happening, would be for our sister to mate. Perhaps this Korlon would stop if she could not be his."

"I had thought of that. Kai is a great warrior and after our discussion at the Yule celebration, I ken he would be a good male for our sister. He also can see her dragon behind her eyes."

"He can?" I questioned. "That is a great gift."

"Aye, Brigid can see mine and our parents see each other's of course." He was prying without prying but I was not ready to tell him yet. I also could see my mate's dragon behind her eyes.

"Aye, good then. Will you tell them?"

Finn nodded and took the deep breath. "We must go to Ireland first and find out if what the male says is true. Then when we return she will be mated."

"But should we leave Tahra alone?" I questioned.

"Kai will not leave her side, of that I am certain, and we will only take your males and a few of mine with us. The rest we leave here to guard the clan."

I nodded slowly. All the princes commanded twenty dragons each. Finn commanded fifty when he was prince and heir. When Bearcbhan and Nameless died, Finn and I split command of their warriors until he became king. As king, he commanded them all but still gave me control over my forty. Thinking of Nameless caused a worrisome thought to enter my mind.

"Finn," I gave it voice. "Have you thought of the males. Nameless commanded? Have they been questioned to see if they knew anything about his betrayal? And have you thoroughly checked their loyalty?"

"Aye, I have. Da' and I spoke to each in turn. There was no indication they knew anything of his plan. They all agreed he was a fairly terrible leader and they had no loyalty to him. He apparently never participated in drills nor went on the patrol with them. To be honest with you, they were not sorry to see him go. They are loyal to us."

"Good," I answered.

"Aye," Finn grinned. "Now, do you want to tell me what is going on with you?"

"What do you mean?"

"Come now, brother," he went on. "I know you better than most. Though I appreciated your dragon's outburst earlier with the male, what is truly causing your ire?"

I did not answer immediately.

"Is it something to do with Sybine? I ken you questioned doing the right thing, but I assure you, you did. Has something happened?"

"In a manner," I admitted.

"If you would confide in me, your secrets will be as mine."

"I ken," I huffed. "I suppose—"

"Finn, Cahal!" Brigid's voice broke from the keep. Finn whipped around so quickly I was surprised he did not lose his balance.

"Brigid, love? What is wrong?" he demanded rushing to her. She looked past him to me and my stomach instantly fell.

"'Tis Sybine," she said holding her husband's arm as Finn wrapped it protectively around her. "She is weeping. I heard her through the door as I was checking on Tahra. Erina and Edan are trying to get in to see what is wrong but the door is barred."

I knew it was futile, I had barred it myself. No one could get in. But Sybine weeping? Why? What happened? My dragon itched and paced in my mind eager to fly to her side.

"Please, Cahal," Brigid held Finn's hand as she stepped closer to me. "She'll make herself sick."

I needed no further motivation. I looked at Finn who nodded then I shifted as fast as I could, my tunic and plaid in tatters. Jumping into the air, my beast beat his wings as fast and as powerfully as we could. The only way into my room with the door barred would be by way of the balcony. I pushed my dragon to go faster and soon we landed on the balustrade, the balcony door still open and I could hear her.

Sybine was weeping.

Still laying on the bed where I left her, she was curled up on her side.

I hurried to the bed not bothering to cover my nakedness as my only concern in that moment, was her welfare.

What happened? My dragon demanded. *Is she injured? Did someone come in and hurt her? I will tear them scale from scale!*

Enough, I bellowed in my mind to silence the creature. *I cannae concentrate on her with you banging on. I sense no wound.*

Hold her to us. I need to feel her.

I gently turned her over so I could cradle her, checking to make sure she was not injured. But when her watery eyes met mine, she searched my face. My dragon still paced in the back of my mind, itching to destroy whatever it was that had hurt her. She stared at me for a long moment then burst into another round of tears. I was helpless. I did not know what I did nor did I ken how to help her.

"Cahal?" I heard Finn's voice as he knocked calmly on the door. "Are you there? Is everything all right?"

Relief rushed through me and I raced to the door. Removing the bar, it swung open and instantly I remembered I was nude after my shift. Covering the important parts with my hands after seeing my mother and Brigid look away, I looked back at Sybine who continued to cry.

"Please," I begged. It shamed me to not know how to calm my own mate, but I could not help her. I stepped aside and the females rushed to Sybine who latched onto their embrace. Da' grabbed a plaid hanging over the back of my chair and handed it to me. Quickly covering, I spoke to Finn and da'.

"I could not see nor sense any injury. She looked at me when I came in and wept even more. As if I scared her. I should never have done this." I turned toward my brother. "Finn, please, annul this mating. She does nae want me and I will nae have her scared of me."

"I cannae," Finn replied in a voice I've heard used on wild animals.

"You can!" I shouted. "We have nae consummated our mating!"

"But you have been with her in the past, lad." Da' stepped forward. "That is why Finn's hands are tied. There is no way."

"I should never have done this!" Anger coursed through me and in a heated moment, I threw my fist against the stone wall beside the door. The shock of the bones in my hand breaking felt good.

Only too late did the sheer silence in the room echo in my ears. My hand ached but the bones already began to knit back together. Once I heard the silence, I turned. Everyone stared at me, even Sybine, who had blessedly, stopped crying. My chest heaved with exertion, pain, and adrenaline, as I looked from one to the other. No one moved and shame curled my belly. Brigid slowly got to her feet from comforting Sybine. Finn took a step toward her, but she stopped him with a hand raised. She came up to me and stared into my eyes.

"Dragon," she spoke in a soothing voice. "I need to speak with Cahal. You both need my healing. Can you let him speak to me?"

Only then did I realize why everyone was staring. My dragon had taken over, my eyes slitted, and I did not know. It was dangerous to have the dragon in control of our bodies when not in dragon form, but to not realize my dragon had taken over was even more perilous. It was called going rogue.

Coaxing my dragon to give me control again, I played on his loyalty to our queen and her unborn whelp. He would never hurt her nor our future king or queen. He easily slid to the back of my mind and I looked down at Brigid, in control once more.

Brigid was standing before me, no fear in her eyes but I felt Finn's energy next to me. His concern for his mate radiated from him. Not since I had gone rogue five years ago had I felt that sort of complete takeover as if I was still in control, but not.

"I am sorry," I said and looked toward my mother, holding Sybine.

"Let me see your hand, Cahal," Brigid ordered with her no-nonsense healer voice.

I acquiesced and let her prod my broken flesh. The pain radiated up my wrist when she touched a particularly tender spot, and I winced. Glancing back to where I had thrown my fist into the wall, debris from the stone littered the floor. A gaping hole was left in the wall. My dragon had punched through the stone? I wondered. His scales must have protected me from most of the damage.

"'Tis already healing," Brigid finally pronounced. "You should be healed by dawn."

"I thank you, my Queen," I bowed out of respect and not knowing what else to do. Again, taking in the faces near me, I looked down and murmured, "forgive me for causing pain or fear. I will sleep in the barracks with my warriors for the few short hours before dawn. That is, if you still want me to accompany you, my king."

"That has not changed, Cahal," Finn answered and squeezed my shoulder.

I bowed to him and sent a final look to my parents. A long look at Sybine, showed her eyes wide with... a nameless emotion, possibly fear and my gut clenched.

I left my room and walked stiffly toward the barracks. Several of the males I commanded were alert instantly, a trait I demanded, as I open the door. When they saw it was me, I noticed confusion flicker across their faces as it was still technically my mating night and I should be with my bride, but they said nothing. I took the extra plaid one of them offered me. Finding an empty birth, I lay down, stuffing a bag of hay beneath my head and closing my eyes, but I found no sleep that night.

Chapter Nine

I opened my eyes to a nudge on my leg. Looking up, my brother's face came into focus.

"Tis dawn," Finn said softly.

I nodded and accepted his hand to help me stand. My body ached from lying on the dirt floor of the barracks.

Finn didn't immediately drop his grasp on my wrist and he took a deep breath. "I am sorry this happened, Cahal," he said. Looking anywhere but at the pity in his eyes, I glanced around to see the warriors who slept after changing the guard a few hours ago. "If I could change it, I would. I ken how difficult it is for you."

"It is what it is," I answered.

"I know Sybine is grieving, we all are. Perhaps given time?"

I shook my head. "It is nae that," I revealed.

Finn studied me. "Then what?"

"It is my fault," I blurted.

"How so?" Finn's brow furrowed in doubt.

"My king," Drake called and popped his head into the barracks. Seeing us, he bowed. "Forgive me. The males are ready, should I have them hold?"

"Aye, for a short time," Finn said. "Be sure we are not disturbed."

"I will, sire." Drake nodded to me, bowed to Finn, and left the barracks.

Once we were alone, Finn moved to the passage in the sidewall. "Come with me," he said and soon we were walking through one of the many natural caves in the mountain.

Having explored them all as lads, we both knew where we were going. Coming to the stairs, we climbed quickly and when we reached the top, Finn pushed open the door to one of the stealth overlooks that surrounded our castle. Walking forward we stood in the early morning sunlight, looking out onto our land. I filled my lungs with the sweet morning air and closed my eyes, feeling the warmth of the sun on my face. It was a long moment before Finn spoke.

"I brought Brigid here nearly a year ago now. Her first moment on our lands and already she had stuck her wee dagger in my shoulder, pummeled my chest with her fists, and screamed at me demanding to be released." He chuckled. "Now look at us."

"A true love match," I agreed. "I am happy for you, Finn."

"It did nae start that way. She told me she wanted to leave, even confessed just recently she thought of befriending you in your state of anger and after finding common ground with you, was going to ask you to steal her away back to her cottage on Lewis land."

"I never would have done that, Finn. I hope you know that."

"I do," Finn assured. "But what I am trying to say is that though it looked hopeless early on, Brigid and I are so very happy now." He turned to me and placed his hand on my shoulder. "It will all get better, Cahal." The confidence in his voice and eyes made my dragon look away. "Sybine is grieving, and you are giving her the space she needs."

"Not really," I mumbled but Finn's grip on my shoulder increased and I was forced to look at him.

"Are you saying you..."

Heaving a sigh, I thrust my hands through my hair. "We kissed," I admitted

"Kissing is good," Finn smirked.

I felt fourteen again as I admitted, "it led to more."

"More? As in?"

"We did not... Not what you're thinking. She..."

"Speak, Cahal, you will have no judgement from me."

"She called out for Bearcbhan."

Finn's face went ashen, and he took a slow steady breath, something he learned from our father.

"How far have you gotten?"

"Far enough, but neither of us were without clothes if that helps you form the image in your mind. After that... I stopped."

"Of course. I understand why. Cahal, I am sorry."

"It brought it all back. Aye, I kenned they were intimate. But I did nae expect the female I love, my true mate, to moan my dead brother's name as I kissed and touched her."

Finn stared at me incredulously. "Your true mate?" He questioned.

"Aye," I confessed. "I see her dragon behind her eyes."

"Oh, Cahal," he breathed and squeezed my shoulder in sympathy. "I am so very sorry. I did not know."

"It was torture to fly away both five years ago and again last eve but..."

"You are an honorable male."

"She begged me to stay beside her last evening before Tahra was taken. I thought we had come to an understanding, a truce of sorts and when we kissed, I got carried away. She had every right to weep last night. I must have scared her. It is my fault."

"From what I gathered last eve after you left... How's your hand by the way?"

I flexed the appendage and though it was tight, the pain was gone. Finn watched and nodded.

"From what I gathered last eve," he said again. "She was the one who initiated your... entanglement and felt guilty for giving into her needs and feelings when she promised to mourn Bearcbhan properly. You have history. 'Tis clear she still cares deeply for you and when a female loves, she will do anything for her male, and desires to show him her love. I still donnae understand why they mated so quickly. If they had just waited..."

"She thought she was carrying my whelp," I confessed. "And I was named War Chief, an unmateable position. She had no choice. Had they not mated, she would have been shunned."

Finn's eyes grew wide. "Adair and Brogan are yours?"

"Nay," I replied quickly. "She was faithful to Bearcbhan and the timing does nae work. They are barely four. Nay, she believed she was carrying and when Bearcbhan found her in the garden, she told him everything. At that time, she did not know da' had given his permission for me to mate. When she found out she wasn't carrying, she realized she had made a mistake but thought of how the clan would view her, pitting one brother against the other... She stayed mated to Bearcbhan. Though, I do believe she always loved me, she loved Bearcbhan too. And misses him greatly."

"So last eve, she was mourning and feeling guilty about your..."

"Mistake," I stated. "It was a mistake, nothing more. It was a mistake to step forward and claim her as mate, but I could not stand aside and watch my true mate marry someone else again."

"Understandable," Finn looked out to the land before us. The dramatic views, the cliffs, crags, flatlands, and rivers. It was another long moment before he spoke again. "What about your dragon?" He finally asked, not looking away from the view before him. "I have never seen a male, nor indeed a female, punched through stone. Scales appeared on your arm and hand as if you were wearing chainmail. You spoke as a human, but your eyes were dragon. Classic signs of a rogue dragon. I need to know… Are you in control?"

"Aye," I answered. "I will admit, I have not had that experience in many years. But I assure you, my dragon is as loyal to you and Brigid as I am."

Finn nodded slowly. "I do not envy you, Cahal. I am proud to call you my brother. But I do not envy you."

"Nor I you, my *king*," I teased.

The corner of Finn's mouth ticked up. "I also need to know," he began, serious once more. "If Uncle Rexian is behind this, where do your loyalties lie?"

"Always with you," I vowed, then knelt and pulled out my dagger. Finn turned to me and waited. I placed the tip of the dirk over my heart, the hilt out to him. "I swear on the iron I hold, if I ever give you cause to question my loyalty, may this blade pierce my heart. I pledge my fealty to you. If I ever break your trust or this bond, I hope this dirk will pierce my heart. For death is a greater gift than disloyalty to you, my king. I am your servant. My pledge is my bond. I swear it to you."

Finn placed a hand on my shoulder in a gesture of acceptance. "And happily, I accept, Cahal. I could not bear to lose another brother."

My chest ached with our mutual pain reflected in his

eyes. Where once there was four, now only two remained.

"Have no fear, my brother," I stood and offered my arm in a warrior shake. "You will never lose me."

Taking my arm, Finn clasped his hand around my wrist and drew me into an embrace.

"Brigid and I will help you and Sybine in anyway we can," he whispered in my ear. Then, pulling back, he kept our arms linked and smiled. "Now, let us go so we can hurry home. I donnae want to be parted from my mate for very long, and we will have a mating to celebrate upon our return."

"Truly?" I asked.

"Aye, Kai found me earlier this morning. He and Tahra spoke last evening and she agreed. Da' and I are happy to accept his suit for our sister's hand."

"I am pleased, and happily accept it as well."

"Hopefully upon our return, my mate and our mother will have assisted Sybine in her grief and helped her come to terms with her desire for you. None of us are blind, Cahal, she wanted you but feared the situation. Brigid has promised to help her, talk to her, and lend advice. Hopefully when you return, your true mate will be waiting for you."

I forced my smile, but I was not going to celebrate just yet.

Chapter Ten

Sybine

Still mortified by what had happened the night before, I waited with Brigid, Tahra, and Erina. Kai stood near, his eyes darting to Tahra every few seconds and by the smile on both their faces, I assumed we would have a mating ceremony soon. Edan stood before us facing the warriors, his back to us.

We waited for Finn and Cahal. According to Drake, they had asked not to be disturbed for a time and I hoped Finn was not chastising Cahal for punching through the wall. Seeing his dragon scales appear and his eyes remained slitted scared me, but not because I was scared *of* him, but *for* him. Though our past and our future was murky, he was always the male I most admired and loved. But with the past the way it was, I kenned he would never accept me. I was thankful he had such restraint, not many males would agree to allow me the time I needed to mourn my mate.

The roar of the crowd jerked me from my thoughts. Finn and Cahal emerged from the barracks and both males look toward us. Finn smiled at Brigid then faced the clan. Cahal locked eyes with me for a brief moment, then stood beside the king. I couldn't blame him for looking away. I had acted reprehensibly.

"Friends," Finn shouted over the din of applause. Everyone quieted as he continued. "I leave the clan in the capable hands of our War Chief and, my soon to be brother-by-mating. When we return, we will have a mating ceremony. Your princess, my sister Tahra, is to mate Chief Kai McKay!" Cheers rang out around us and Tahra beamed as Kai stepped up beside her. Taking his hand, she nodded in thanks to the clan who cheered. The dragon males who are already shifted, tapped their talons on the ground and lifted their heads into the air to blow out fire, a tradition since dragons cannot cheer.

Finn raised a hand to quiet the clan. "We go to find the male who wanted to take the princess against her will. If any of you have information about this please seek Chief MacKay or any other of our trusted guard. Until I see you again, remember *clach forti!*" Finn shouted our clan motto; *With strong claw.* The clan shouted it back and Finn turned to Brigid. She held his gaze and smiled softly. Walking over to her to say goodbye, they spoke low and kissed.

I felt Cahal's eyes on me. It was my duty to send him off. In the eyes of the clan, we were mated. I took one step toward him. His eyes darkened slightly, and he walked over to me quickly.

"I will not trouble you, my lady." His stiff, formal greeting was so unlike him. "I thank you for sending me off in the eyes of the clan. If and when I return, perhaps we can discuss suitable arrangements."

"Arrangements?" I questioned, my voice sticking.

Cahal searched my gaze with an impassive one. "I will not have you scared of me, nor anyone. You need not fear about your whelps. I will look after them as I swore to you."

"What are you saying?"

He huffed a sigh. "I am saying... I donnae ken. If you desire to live cohabitantly, I understand. I cannae deny my... love for you, Sybine. But I would do nothing to hurt you. You have my life oath."

My heart raced. A life oath was rarely given and if broken, a mate could ask for the ultimate punishment. Swallowing against the bile in my throat, I took his hand.

"I thank you for what you have done for my whelps and me."

"It was nothing."

"It was everything, Cahal." I cupped his jaw with my hand and waited until he looked at me. "It has been so long since we..." When I saw his understanding, I continued. "And Bearcbhan was my mate, a good father, and I loved him in my own way but... He was not my true mate. I could never see his dragon behind his eyes, not as I can see yours." His eyes widened but he said nothing. "The reason I wept last night was, I miss him and want to give him the honor of mourning him, but I have missed you too and when I said his name, I knew I ruined our time together. I hope you know... I do want to be with you. Our history is a difficult one, but it is ours and I would never change it. It is difficult for me to be with you thinking... how could you forgive me, but you were and are nothing but wonderful. I hope you ken, I donnae want to be strangers. You are my true mate and I do love you, Cahal. I always have." I leaned forward and kissed him. He did not move. When I pulled back, his eyes searched mine. "I will be waiting for your return, Warrior. And I desire to be as a proper mate to you when you do."

I watched as his throat worked and his face relaxed slightly. "I..." he breathed. "I will return to you, my true mate. For I too, see your dragon and desire to show you how much I love you still."

I smiled as a freeing giddy feeling churned in my chest and belly. "Then hurry home to me, dragonman."

With the final kiss, he walked back to Finn who waited. Without another word, the remaining dragons shifted and took to the air. The thrill of the breeze billowing from the wings, and the excitement knowing, soon, I will give in to what I desired most, rushed through me, making me heady.

Brigid slipped her hand into mine as we watched our mates fly. Turning to my sister-by-mating, I smiled.

"'Tis glad I am you and Cahal have spoken. I hope soon you both will be happy with your choices," she said.

"I believe we will be, my queen."

Brigid squeezed my hand affectionately then turned. "Join me for a respite in my solar?" She addressed Erina, Edan, Tahra, and Kai. "We can perhaps speak of the mating ceremony." My smile grew. Tahra was finally getting her happy beginning with the male she loved.

Before anyone had a chance to speak, Edan walked over to Kai and dropped a heavy hand on his shoulder.

"You lasses go ahead," he said jovially. "Kai and I have some things to discuss." He squeezed Kai's shoulder and Kai tried not to wince, but it was clear he was about to be given the *father of the female* speech. Erina's tinkling laugh came next.

"Be easy on him, Edan," she teased. "Remember you are no longer king. It would not be easy for our son to have to punish you for injuring his War Chief."

"Ah, no injury..." Edan winked. "We're just going to talk."

Kai's face went pale and Tahra's brows drew together in concern, but her mother led her away and into the keep. Edan and Kai followed me into the Great Hall but stopped near the fireplaces as I headed up to the queen's solar.

End of Part One

Part Two

Chapter One

Cahal

Our uncle's kingdom was well fortified. Many generations ago, the Irish dragon king built his fortress in the middle of Lough Leane, the largest lake in Munster Province. The king also burnt all the trees within view on the shore so no human could build ships to attack them. Our Uncle Rexian, the current king had stopped the tradition of burning the woods and as Finn and I walked to the edge of the lough together, I took in the beauty of the young trees, green grass, and purple mountains covered in flowers.

Our warrior males waited for Finn's order but as thirty could be considered a threat, or act of war, Finn turned to them.

"You males stay here and build shelter," he said. "My brother and I will go to our uncle and speak with him. Your *all is well* signal, will be my roar."

Knowing, even in human form Finn's dragon could roar, the males agreed and as they worked to gather some fallen tree limbs, Finn and I shifted and jumped into the air. Flying across the lough, we landed on the steps of the keep rising out of the water.

The doors opened and our uncle's War Chief stood in the entry, flanked by three warriors on either side of him. Finn and I shifted back to our human form.

"Uncle Raeghar," Finn said and nodded in respect, but I was glad to see he remembered his place and did not bow.

"Aodhfionn," Uncle Raeghar began cautiously. "Why have you come to us prepared for battle?"

"We seek an audience with King Rexian," Finn said.

"Is my brother expecting you?"

"He will see us," Finn stated.

Raeghar crossed his arms over his chest. "Will he?" His sarcastic tone was one I had not heard often.

"Careful, Uncle," I stepped forward. "You do not speak to your nephew. You speak to my king."

Uncle Raeghar pulled himself up to his full height,

always the tallest of us all, even Finn who stood nearly halfway over six feet. Our uncle towered over him but bowed in respect.

"My apologies, King Aodhfionn. I will announce you to King Rexian as you prepare yourselves." He turned and gave instruction to the two men standing behind him. "Stay with them."

Though I was pulling on my plaid, I still heard his warning, and it gave me pause.

We waited, saying nothing to each other or our guardians until our uncle returned.

"Rexian will see you."

Finn took a silent breath, but I felt the tension and worry radiating off him. It was only his third day as king and already he had to deal with his brother going rogue; me, our sister being kidnapped, and my mate weeping as if she had lost... well, her mate. I shook my head. Aye, I did nae envy him.

Soon, we rounded the corner and came upon the raised dais in the Great Hall. Our uncle sat on the lone chair. I hesitated to call it a throne as it was a simplistic seat, unlike our grandfather's golden one gilded with precious gems mined from the earth and caves on his land. My lips tipped up slightly when I saw my uncle. His curly hair was as unruly as ever and though he was our mother's eldest brother, his face betrayed little of his age. His tan colored eyes searched our faces as he stood and stepped down from the dais which was against tradition as we were technically visiting dignitaries.

His face split into a grin and his entire countenance welcomed us. "Finn, Cahal, dear gods, it's good to see you, lads." He embraced each of us individually. Holding me at arm's length, he shook his head in disbelief. "You have grown so much,

Cahal. I hardly recognize you! What brings you here?"

"We have had an issue, Uncle. We need to speak to you as a matter of great urgency," Finn answered.

Uncle Rexian's eyes grew wide and he paled slightly. "Your mother? Is she—"

"Nay, have nay fear for Mother, she is well," Finn stated.

Rexian visibly relaxed. "Tahra?"

"While would you ask about our sister?"

Rexian looked between us, confused. "Why wouldn't I? She is as much my sister's blood as you two. Has something happened to her?"

A side door opened and our Uncle Elyan, younger than Rexian but not the youngest of my seven uncles, and Raeghar stepped into the room.

"Ah ha! I heard our nephews had arrived," he cheered and smiled broadly as he embraced us both tightly. "It's good to see you, lads. Is all well? How is everyone?"

"They were about to tell me, brother," Uncle Rexian explained.

My stomach knotted again. Embracing my uncles was like coming home. I had fostered with them for many years when my grandfather was still king and to now suspect them of this foul deed was not sitting well with me.

Elyan continued as if Rexian hadn't spoken. "Gods, I haven't seen you in five years, Finn. Not since..." He broke off and shot a glance at me.

"Not since Sybine's and Bearcbhan's mating ceremony," I supplied.

"Indeed," Elyan looked down sheepishly. Then, his brow furrowed and he looked over at Finn. "We heard of your losses."

Raeghar spoke next. "We are sorry for it."

"Aye, we lost a good warrior," Finn praised. "And an even better brother and male. Bearcbhan's loss is heavy on all our hearts."

"And Teyrnon's," Rexian supplied with a questioning tone.

"Alas, no, Uncle," Finn answered. "It was his treachery that caused my mate to nearly lose her life and our whelp. And it was he who killed our brother. My father's decree was he is to be Nameless. I fully intend to support that now I am king."

"Dear gods… your mother's letters only spoke of the loss, not the subterfuge." Rexian glanced at his two brothers then back at us. "We can imagine your pain, lads. It is never easy with family goes against family."

I bristled at Rexian calling Finn a lad. Me, I understood since I was practically raised by the males in the room, but Finn was king. Before I had a chance to speak to him and remind him of Finn's title, my brother spoke.

"Uncle, as much as I appreciate you and your love for us, I ask in future you respect me is your equal and not as your nephew. I am king now and if I allow even family to classify me as a lad, I will have no hope in maintaining my recognition with others."

"Of course, my apologies. Is Finn still acceptable?"

"Aye, Finn is fine," he agreed.

"In more formal settings, I will remember to use your full name. It is difficult for me as you are my nephew, but I will strive to remember. I understand what it is like to establish yourself as a ruler after such a short time."

"I appreciate your thoughtfulness and acceptance."

"Good. Raeghar, please call for ale and light refreshments. Let us sit and speak of this odd matter further. You still have not answered me regarding Tahra."

"Tahra?" Elyan started. "Why? Has something happened? Is she well? What is wrong?"

"Let us sit as they pour ale," Rexian offered as Raeghar rejoined us from speaking with one of the female servants standing nearby. She had curtsied and left presumably to gather the food and drink.

We followed Uncle Rexian to a set of four chairs. Finn and I took the two opposite Rexian and Elyan as Uncle Raeghar stood between them. His brownish green eyes assessing the situation. His gaze sharp and guarded, he was the only uncle to not greet us with gaiety.

The servant returned with a tray of bread, cheeses, honey, and a pitcher of ale. Once we all had a drink in hand, Finn began speaking.

"Uncles," he said slowly. "Firstly, I need you to all understand we are not accusing anyone of anything." I saw his eyes lock with Raeghar. "We had our males wait on land because we did not want the appearance of an attack."

Rexian sat up and Raeghar widened his stance.

"Finn, dear gods, please tell us what is going on. For I fear, my mind is thinking up all sorts of things." Rexian stated.

Finn took a drink and a deep breath. "Last night or rather early this morning, Tahra was abducted from her room.

Her companion was drugged with dragon bane."

It took only a moment for the realization to settle in and all three males lunged forward, speaking over each other.

"Is she all right?"

"What happened?"

"How did this happen?"

"Where is she now?"

"Is she all right?"

Finn held up his hand stopping their torrent of questions. "Her now betrothed, my War Chief, Kai saw her abductors and flew after them," Finn continued once they had quieted. "He destroyed their ships and helped Tahra escaped before she was violated."

Tension radiated off the three men. Elyan's face went red, and all three's eyes flashed to dragon slits. Eventually, Rexian's body eased enough and his eyes rounded.

"If she is well, why have you come here?" He asked. "It is not for a rescue, nor to destroy the monsters who took her. So why, Finn?"

Finn looked at me and I nodded. "Uncle," he proceeded with caution. "I need to know. Did you have anything to do with it?"

"What?" Rexian asked incredulously. "You cannot be serious."

"Be careful who you accused, nephew," Raeghar's deep voice and slitted eyes were a warning.

Finn looked up at him with equal parts strength and intensity. "I am not the one who has forgotten to whom I speak,

War Chief." He spat the title. Smoke curled beneath Raeghar's nose.

"Please," Elyan spoke up with a quick glance at Raeghar. "Tell us, why do you think we could possibly have anything to do with it." Elyan, the peacemaker, was able to diffuse the situation almost instantly. He was the only one I had seen Raeghar listen to when he was incensed. "You know we all love Tahra."

"There was one male we left alive and when we questioned him, he spoke about working under the orders of the Irish dragon king," I stated. "We, neither of us, think you would want to hurt Tahra. But I... *We* need to know who he meant. You are the last Irish dragon king, Uncle. We came here to see if you knew anything about those men. You can see how it looks."

Rexian and his brothers were quiet for a long moment. Finally, the king leaned forward. "As your uncle, Finn, I give you my solemn vow, I have nothing to do with this. I love Tahra as my own daughter, had I had one. As a king, I offer the only thing I can, a treaty between us, and offer my warriors to assist you in your search. I, too, want to know who is slandering my name. I offer Raeghar's help in any way possible. He will be as your own War Chief."

I glanced up at my uncle to see a sour expression on his face. It was clear he did not like the idea. But could there be guilt there too? I shook my head. Perhaps my own experiences with Nameless had tainted my idea of a brother's loyalty.

"We accept any help you offer," Finn replied. "Have the treaty between us drawn up. I am eager to sign it. I hope you understand my predicament."

"I do, nephew," Rexian stated. "Have no fear. I do not bear you a grudge for asking the difficult questions. This male whoever he is, thought he was working under orders of the king. Well, I can assure you, he was under no orders from me."

"I take you at your word, Uncle. There will be no thought on this again," Finn stood and reached for his arm in a warrior's shake.

A door opened somewhere behind us. I was already on my feet, ready to protect my king when I heard of soft feminine voice and smelled a sweet scent.

"Oh! Forgive me, your majesty. I did nae ken you had company."

I caught sight of the female standing in the shadows when Elyan walked over to her.

"Farrah," he smiled. "Is all well, love?"

"Aye," she replied with an answering grin. "I was looking for you. It was nothing important. Please, do not let me interrupt," the female, Farrah said.

"Not an interruption," Rexian motioned for her to come forward. "Farrah, come meet our nephews."

Elyan and the female walked out of the shadows and Finn and I bowed our heads to her. She was a beautiful female, her advanced years looked well on her. Though hardly old, her blonde hair was greying, and her eyes held lines of laughter around them. I estimated she was no more than forty-five in human years. Her blue eyes sparkled as she curtsied to us.

"Elyan has spoken of you often," she greeted. "Permit me to guess your names?"

Finn inclined his head in agreement and smirked. "My mate enjoys guessing games as well, my lady. Please continue."

She observed us both with a keen gaze. "You are Finn,"

she said to him and then her eyes looked to me. "And you must be Cahal. Your eyes remind me so much of Raeghar's." she glanced over at the War Chief who kept his expression blank.

Rexian stood to Finn's other side and chuckled. "Indeed, sister, this is my nephew Aodhfionn, King of the Mackay Dragons, and leader of the Lewis clan; and my nephew Cahal, his brother and most trusted advisor."

"My Lords," she curtsied to us. The only thing marring her delicate features was a massive light pink scar crisscrossing her face from under the hairline to her right, across her brow and nose, down her left cheek and ending at her jaw. A peak of burned flesh appeared at her neck and the stippling of the flesh was something I had seen many a time.

"My lady," Finn replied. "I did not realize..." He looked to our uncles with a questioning gaze.

Elyan spoke next. "Forgive me, I forgot you did not know. Connifarrah is my mate."

"Oh," Finn's brow rose in surprise. "I had not heard. Congratulations, Uncle. When did this happy event occur?"

"We celebrate two years next month," Elyan said placing a kiss on Connifarrah's hair. "Our meeting was five years ago just after Bearcbhan and Sybine..."

My spine still stiffened and when I heard their names together. Though I knew it was silly, I could nae stop it.

"Elyan was my savior," Farrah revealed. "I was injured, and he found me."

"Indeed," Elyan agreed. "She had been hit and lay on the forest floor."

"I thought it was a dream, but I remembered flying." The

affection in her tone put me at ease.

"Where in our country are you from, my lady?" Finn asked.

"Skye," she answered.

"Ah, beautiful isn't it? Tell me, have you had a chance to see Skara Brea? It's exquisite and just north of Cairns."

I kept my face neutral. Finn was testing her. Skara Brea was far north on Orkney Island, one of the islands near Norway.

"Oh aye beautiful," she answered. And just like that, the ease I felt vanished. She had never been to our isle.

"Remember love, the Skara Brea is in the northern islands. We went together a few months ago," Elyan stated with a sharp look at Finn.

"Oh, aye, of course," she breathed. "Forgive me, I sometimes get confused."

"You will stay with us? Have dinner? You are welcome for however long," Rexian spoke next, no doubt attempting to change the subject of conversation. "We can tell you more of Connifarrah's ordeal."

"Indeed, our thanks, Uncle," Finn replied.

"I will have your rooms prepared," Rexian motioned to one of the servants who curtsied. "They will connect via a mutual door. If you have need to speak to each other without ears, I hope that will suffice."

"We appreciate your hospitality," I said.

"I will assist," Connifarrah offered and with a kiss on Elyan's cheek and a curtsey to Rexian and Finn, she walked to the stairs and out of our sight.

"A word, nephew," Elyan said to Finn. Never in my life had I heard him use such a tone and my dragon scales itched under my skin. "I don't know what sort of game you intended on playing, but leave my mate alone. She has already gone through so much. My word should be vow enough for you to believe she is who she says she is."

"There are many taken in by a pretty face," Finn countered. "I am looking for a traitor and know nothing of this female."

Raeghar stepped forward but Elyan held up a hand. "I can fight my own battles, Rae." Then looking at us, he continued. "Connifarrah was tortured and nearly killed while under the command of her former leader. She suffers from memory loss and for you to try and trick her is beneath you, nephew."

"Be careful of your tone, Uncle," I warned.

"Shall we perhaps have some music?" Rexian offered.

"I love you, lads you know that, but she is my mate. I am protective of her. She has given you no cause to suspect her. I am asking you to please, leave her out of this."

Finn was quiet for a long moment before he nodded once. "I will apologize to your mate, Uncle. I trust no newcomer. And my suspicion of family stems from our own past with Nameless. Forgive me, this is not the reunion I was hoping for."

Elyan offered his arm in a warrior's shake. "All is forgiven, Finn. Now, tell us the news of our sister. How does she fare?"

And with that, we were ushered to the seats again and more ale was poured. Our uncles were goodhearted, and they had soft spots for us. But as we laughed about something my father did to cause our mother to blow a fireball on his arse when they were shifted just the other day, I noticed Raeghar's face. It was stoic. No emotion reflected in his eyes. I was used to that as I studied under him as a lad. He took his duty as War Chief very seriously. What worried me were the quick glances he made up the stairs and around the room to the warriors he had stationed by the doorway. A blonde haired warrior locked eyes with him for a brief moment and, as if they were communicating, he nodded and left his post when Connifarrah returned and went to the kitchens. The blonde male followed her and stood at the door of the kitchen, his back to us. Protecting her.

The hair on the back of my neck stood on end. What was Raeghar hiding?

Chapter Two

Finn and I were escorted up to our rooms near the front of the keep, overlooking the lough and our warriors beyond. As soon as we were alone, we opened the door joining our rooms and Finn went to the window. Once our males signaled back at all was well, Finn sat on the bed in a huff.

"I do wish da' was here," he said.

"You are doing wonderfully, Finn. You are showing your strength. It is needed."

Quiet for a moment, my brother finally looked up at me. "What is your opinion on this?"

"On which part?" I questioned

"All of it," he replied. "Did you notice anything?"

I debated. On one hand, I wasn't certain what I saw was anymore than a War Chief concerned over one of his clanmates. On the other, the looks between Raeghar and Connifarrah when they thought no one was looking concerned me.

"I see you saw something, brother," Finn said. "Why do you hesitate to tell me?"

"What I saw I do not believe affects us. But I hesitate because I am unsure of what it is I actually saw."

"I did not believe you when you first came to me about Nameless, I will not make the same mistake again. Tell me."

"I had no evidence when it came to Nameless and I did not tell you enough to act upon, the fault is no one's. Besides, I was still fighting being rogue. I do not believe you did not believe me, you were merely unsure."

"That's generous of you," Finn replied. "Still, you can tell me anything, brother. I will believe you."

I huffed. "I saw a look between our uncle's mate Connifarrah and our uncle... Raeghar."

"Raeghar?" He questioned. "Odd. And this look was clearly disturbing or else you would not have noticed."

"I wouldn't say disturbing, but strange. They were

sneaking glances when no one was looking and then after she left to prepare our rooms I noticed him communicate to another and that warrior would not leave her side. I am uncertain as to why he would feel the need to protect her from us."

"Could they be... carrying on with each other?"

"I hope not for Uncle Elyan's sake, but... I cannae say no. I would like to follow them, see if they reveal more of their relationship."

"Do," Finn stated. "I would join you but your absence I can explain, both of us would be difficult. Be careful."

"I will be. Let us go down for dinner." I moved back to the door connecting our two rooms when I paused and turned back to Finn. "I noticed how you did not mention Korlon. Was there a reason?"

"Aye," he replied. "I intend to bring it up in passing to see how they react."

"I see. I will not mention it then."

"My thanks," Finn forced a smile. The look in his eye gave me pause.

"You miss your mate," I surmised.

Finn nodded. "Am I so readable?"

"Nay, but I ken the look."

"I worry overmuch," he went on. "I have a feeling something is going to change and I cannae tell if it is for good or ill."

"All will be well, Finn."

"I pray you are right." Finn smiled slightly. "Come, let us go down to dinner. When she leaves the Hall, make some excuse, and follow her.

"I will. I do not like how we did nae ken of their mating. And how quickly Elyan's temperament changed when you questioned her."

"I agree. Being human she is most likely a Lewis and that worries me. Could she be loyal to the Laird?" Finn questioned.

"We learn nothing from staying up here," I offered. "Let's go down." The first few strains of lute music drifted up from beneath us. "It sounds like our Uncle is giving us the royal welcome. Song and dance, good food and ale."

"Aye," Finn stood and walked to his trunk that two of our males had brought over from the palette we had used to transport it and pulled out a fresh tunic and plaid. "I do wish I could jump into the lough and cleanse the grime of travel off my skin." He stripped off his tunic and walked over to the vanity.

"I could call for a bath to be brought, if you want," I offered, though my first instinct was to tease my brother.

"And have you and our uncles tease me mercilessly?" he poured water and dipped one of the strips of linen into it. "No thank you. I will suffice with a strip of linen and this pitcher of water."

I grinned. "It would only be a small tease." Finn threw the wet linen at me. I chuckled and dodged. "Oh come now, is that any way to treat your poor brother?"

"My arse," he grumbled but wet another and passed the cloth over his torso. I hurried to my room and did the same. Once fresh, dressed, and ready to face the *cèilidh*, I looked back over to Finn's door and saw him standing, leaning against the doorway.

"What?" I questioned.

"I wanted to say thank you, brother. I am glad to have you with me."

"I am glad to be here, Finn."

Then, Finn did something neither of us had done in a long time. He walked over to me and pulled me into an embrace. Stunned at first, I reciprocated, thumping him on the back. When we pulled away, his eyes were lighter.

"Now, the sooner we learn what happened here, the sooner we can get back to our mates. Come."

"You said the right thing," I smiled. "Lead the way."

Finn and I walked out of our rooms and headed down the passage and to the Great Hall below.

Finn

Sitting in my uncle's Great Hall surrounded by my family, I hated the niggling feeling of suspicion. Meeting with Rexian, Raeghar, and Elyan, three of the saner uncles according to Cahal, had gone better than expected. As the meal was cleared from the table, dancing began and Rexian asked me to join him at the chairs by the fire.

Feeling Cahal's eyes on me, I moved with my uncle and accepted his offered cup of whiskey. We said nothing for a while, simply watching the dancers, but soon, Rexian's voice came to my ears low and soft.

"I know what it is like, Finn."

Turning to him, I raised my eyebrows. "What *what* is like, Uncle?"

"What it is you are feeling. Going through. I was

blessedly older than you are now when I took my father's mantle of leadership. But even then, I felt the burdens of kingship. If you ever need to speak with someone about your thoughts, please know, I am here."

"I thank you for your offer, Uncle. There have been times where I questioned myself and if I am making the correct decisions, but I, like you, are fortunate enough to still have my father living."

"Aye, that is fortunate indeed for you," he said, though his voice was tight as he spoke.

"Speaking of," I looked around the Great Hall. "Where is my grandfather? I expected to see him here."

Rexian's grip on his cup grew tighter. "Father is... indisposed. I have sent him to check on our northern border with my brother Velkin."

"I see," I answered. Then my eyes were drawn to movement to my left, near the dais. Connifarrah walked past Raeghar and their eyes met. My eyes flickered to Elyan who laughed jovially at something my cousin, Cinaeth, Rexian's eldest, said. Cahal caught my eyes and nodded.

"Uncle, what is the story of Connifarrah and Elyan? Their mating is sudden, is it no'?"

"Not at all," Rexian stated. "Connifarrah has been with the clan for nearly five years. She and my mate were great friends."

"Where is my aunt? I have missed her," I asked. Rexian said nothing but the look in his eyes made me bite back the words. "Oh dear gods, Uncle. Donnae say it is what I fear."

He nodded. "Three months ago, now." The pain in his voice tore at me. "It was a complication with our whelp."

I felt my stomach pitch. That was my greatest fear with Brigid. "Uncle, I am so very sorry. Why did you no' tell us?"

He shrugged. "I knew you were getting the clan back to functioning. You did not need to mourn another."

"We would have mourned with you."

"And you had two others to mourn, as well as transition into kingship and making sure the Lewis clan was benevolent."

"But we are family," I argued.

He looked at me for a long moment before speaking. "Aye, we are."

His words struck at the nerve I had clearly injured with my suspicion. "Uncle... I—"

"I shall retire to my room, if that is acceptable," Cahal's voice cut me off. Looking over at my brother, I saw that determined look in his eyes. Connifarrah had retired and he was eager to watch her door and follow her if she left.

"Of course," Rexian said. "Though it is early, you must have had a long journey."

"I am tired, and my mate makes it very difficult to sleep."

"Your mate? You mated Sybine after all?"

"She is still of age to bear whelps. It is clan tradition," he justified.

"Of course. You didn't an admirable thing, Cahal. If I had known I would have raised a toast to you this eve."

"I thank you, but it was unnecessary."

"Tomorrow then. Sleep well, nephew."

Cahal looked over at me and I nodded. He would report

back later that evening. He bowed to us both and headed across the Hall and up the stairs.

"Come, Finn, a game of chess?"

"I would be delighted. Never have I met a match quite like you, Uncle." I grinned at him as he walked us over to his chessboard and refilled our cups with more whiskey.

Chapter Three

Cahal

Keeping to the shadows, I waited down the hall from Elyan's and Connifarrah's room. Seeing my uncle in the Great Hall speaking with my cousin; Rexian's son and heir, before I left, I knew he would not be seeking his bed anytime soon.

Movement from the far end of the hallway caught my

126

attention and I ducked back into the alcove before I was seen. Peeking out when I felt all was safe, I watched a figure, dressed in a long black cloak knock twice at the bedchamber door. It opened and I caught sight of Connifarrah wearing a long brown cloak.

"Are you sure about this?" the voice was Raeghar's, deeper than the others even when quiet and his tall form dwarfed the doorway.

"Aye, it is the only way." The soft feminine voice of Connifarrah came next.

"I don't like lying to him, Conni," Raeghar said.

"I know, but I have to do this and he cannae find out."

"Then we need to hurry."

"I am ready."

Again, I ducked into the darkness as Connifarrah lifted the hood of her cloak as Raeghar shut the door behind her. She started down the hallway.

"Nay, this way. Out the back. It is the only way he won't see us," Raeghar stated.

There was a pause and the scent of fear drifted to my nose. "Tell me I am doing the right thing, Rae please." Her voice trembled.

"I cannot do that," Raeghar said. "But know I am by your side, always."

"You mean so much to me. Thank you for everything."

"Come now, we must hurry."

From my hiding place, I watched them hurry past in black cloaks. Raeghar paused a moment, near my alcove, but I had made sure to mask my scent by dousing my tunic in lemon water and rubbing garlic on my arms. The pungent odor of the root would be chalked up to smells from the kitchen at dinner and lemons were one of the things dragons could not smell.

"What is it?" Connifarrah asked anxiously.

He tilted his head, and his eyes flashed a dragon slits to try and see in the dark. Fortunately, I was enough behind the alcove wall that he could not see me.

"Raeghar?" She questioned.

"Nothing," he answered. "I thought... It's nothing, let's go."

They fled down the back stairs and out the kitchen door. I followed at a safe distance. I kept to the shadows and watched as my uncle pulled off his cloak and tunic, handing it to Connifarrah on the steps. He jumped into the water surrounding the keep and shifted. His large silver dragon floated on the still lough. Folding up his cloak and tunic and putting them into the bag she carried, Connifarrah took hold of the scales on his shoulder near his wing and swung one leg over his neck, as if straddling a horse. I had seen Finn carry Brigid that way before. Raeghar did not move until she was situated.

Finally, she leaned down and spoke softly into his ear. "Fly, Rae."

With a nod of his head, he swam a little further out and with the help of his massive wings, he flew into the air.

Once they were far enough away, I pulled out of my own tunic, hid it in the shadows and shifted. Flying straight up into the night sky, I caught up with them and coasted high above in the darkness. My black scales hiding me from their view.

We didn't fly far, but we were outside my uncle's

territory. I watched as Raeghar landed in a grove and helped Connifarrah down from his neck. She still held the bag with his tunic and cloak. Shifting quickly, my uncle grabbed the tunic and pulled it over his head, then tied the cloak in place around his shoulders. Taking her hand, he hurried to the north.

Once I was certain I would not be discovered, I landed and shifted, catching their scent easily. Stalking through the woods, I prayed no one was around and my nakedness would go unnoticed.

Finally, their scent grew stronger, and I slowed, careful where I placed my feet. Fortunately up wind, they would not catch me, and I watched.

Raeghar and Connifarrah stood in a clearing, waiting. Their backs were to me and my eyes moved past them for any movement to the north.

"You are sure this is correct?" She asked my uncle, her worried voice loud in the still night.

"Aye, the clearing just north of the border. This is the place," Raeghar confirmed.

Connifarrah wrung her hands. "Then where is she?" She demanded.

"We must have patience. The moon is not yet to the top of the trees."

"And yet you are early." I was instantly on alert as an elderly voice seemed to come from all around us.

Connifarrah stepped forward. "Please, you are my only hope. I need your help," Connifarrah spoke in the darkness.

"Have you the payment, child?" Again, the voice came from no one place in particular.

Raeghar pulled out a pouch and held it out. "Not until we get what you need. Show yourself, hag."

There was no reply and every sound went silent. The hair on my arms stood on end and my scales rubbed just below the surface of my skin. But I never lowered my gaze from the two figures in the middle of the glen.

Slowly, a hunched figure walked out of the woods in front of Raeghar. A dark cloak hid their features, but the old, gnarled hand clasped around a crooked white staff and it was the only thing showing that it was human, or at least had skin; for I very much doubted it was *human*.

Raeghar's hand shot out to grab Connifarrah's arm and pushed her behind him. The cloaked figure reached them and stood before them. For a moment, they just stared at each other until Connifarrah tentatively stepped around Raeghar and faced the figure.

The hand not holding the staff, produced a vial and offered it to Connifarrah. She took it almost reverently.

"Two drops in food daily and all your problems will disappear," the voice said.

"Does it matter what time of day?" Connifarrah asked.

"Just before bed is best."

"How long until I know it's working?"

"You'll know," the figure said.

"Thank you," she clutched it to her chest and nodded to Raeghar who offered the pouch. The tinkling sound told me it was coins.

"Also," the figure spoke again as it tucked the pouch away into the folds of its cloak. "It would help to add a little blood of the one or a relative." It looked at Raeghar.

"Why?" He demanded.

"More potent. But not essential."

In a blink, the... *it* was gone. Connifarrah looked up at Raeghar, pleadingly.

"No, Connie," he stated. "I agreed to bring you here but not this."

"Please, Rae, you heard her. It's more potent."

"I am a dragon. Do you know what my blood could do? I won't risk it. Now, let us get you back before he misses you."

Raeghar pulled off his cloak and began to remove his tunic, when Connifarrah sobbed and looked away.

"What is wrong?" He demanded immediately on alert.

She shook her head, but the tears kept falling. I took a deep breath, but it wasn't fear I smelled, it was desperation. The scents were similar, but fear had more of a tanginess to it. Raeghar pulled her to him, her head barely coming to his mid chest. She was not a small woman in height, but my uncle was the tallest of us all.

"What is it?" He asked gently.

"What if it doesn't work?" She sobbed.

"It will," he soothed.

"After everything... I could never face it if it didn't."

"Worrying about it will only make it worse. Now, dry your tears. If it will make you feel better, I will give you some of my blood."

She looked up at him. "You will?"

"Aye, here." He pulled away from her, motioned for her to open the stopper in the vial and took his knife. I heard the tear of flesh and immediately scented blood but it was mixed with a strong scent of whatever was in the vial. It was earthy, pungent but not altogether unpleasant. After a couple drops of Raeghar's blood, the scent changed. It was much more fragrant and smelled of petrichor.

Connifarrah placed the stopper on the vial and Raeghar retracted his finger which no doubt was already healed. She threw her arms around his waist and thanked him.

"You are welcome, but now, we must go."

And that was my cue to leave. Quickly and silently, I hurried to the west and shifted once I saw Raeghar's silver dragon take flight. I climbed high into the sky and followed.

Chapter Four

Finn

I paced in my room. Cahal was taking far too long and nearly all in the keep was asleep. Soon though, I heard the soft flap of dragon wings. Stepping out to our shared balcony, I watched as my brother's black dragon form slowly descended from the sky and landed before me.

"I was worried," I said as he quickly shifted.

"I had to be sure they did not see me. I hung back until I saw them disappear and watched the light extinguish in Raeghar's room."

"So Raeghar is in league with Connifarrah? What did you see?" I asked, allowing him to come inside and offering him a glass of whiskey as he pulled on a tunic.

"I am unsure," he answered happily accepting the whiskey. "What I saw could be taken one way, easily, but I could be wrong. Looks are deceiving."

"Aye, we know that well," I agreed. "But tell me, what did you see?"

He proceeded to tell me what happened in the glen and I agreed, it looked suspicious, but could also be something else.

"I never felt such power. Whatever it was, was ancient," he explained speaking of the entity who gave Connifarrah the vial.

"A druid or a witch perhaps," I offered.

"I suppose. My main question is, what is the purpose of the vial? Do they mean harm to Uncle Elyan?"

"That is not a question we can answer alone," I stated. Cahal huffed a sigh. "What is it, brother?" I asked. "Speak freely."

"No matter what the end result is with their midnight escapade, I do believe Rexian should be told, but if it is nothing, I do not want to make an enemy of Raeghar."

"I agree. But secret meetings with witches, and I used the term carefully as Brigid was accused of being one, should not go undiscovered. We should go speak with the king."

Cahal nodded and downed the whiskey. Standing, he followed me down the hall to the king's chamber. I knocked twice and listened. The sound of rustling parchments and heavy footsteps echoed behind the door. The bolt slid back, and the door opened.

"Finn? Cahal?" Our uncle questioned. "Come in, lads, 'tis past the witching hour."

We stepped into the room, taking in the changes. Usually bright and cheerful, the room was grey and quiet. Dried, shriveled flowers were still in a vase on our aunt's vanity, dust had accumulated on the table."

"Oh, forgive me, it is a force of habit to call you lads as I was there for your births. Forgive me. Can I offer you something to drink?"

Cahal looked around the room his eyes resting on the unused vanity. "Uncle," he breathed. "Why didn't you tell me?"

Rexian swallowed and turned away slightly, hiding his tears. "There was much going on."

"The whelp?" Cahal asked hopefully.

He shook his head and Cahal took a deep breath, tears instantly shimmered in his dark eyes. I had misjudged their connection. It ran deeper. Almost as a father and a son. Rexian cleared his throat and turned back to us. I saw the tears swimming in his light eyes. He pushed a hand through his brown curly hair.

"I tell you this," he began, forcing a watery smile. "I do not wish losing their true mate on anyone."

My stomach pitched and I swallowed the bile that instantly filled my mouth. Rexian turned and poured three cups of whiskey. Turning back to us, he offered the drink. Tossing his back in one go, I understood the pain, but I was able to return to my mate. Looking over at Cahal, I realized with the start what sort of pain he endured when Sybine married our brother. It brought my world into focus.

"Uncle, we are deeply sorry for your loss. But there is a reason for our visit this late," I said.

"Of course," he answered and motioned to the chairs by the fireplace. His orange fire blazing in the hearth. Cahal stood looking around the room for another chair. His eyes lightened on the desk at the far wall. "May I?" He asked.

"Of course," Rexian agreed and Cahal pulled the chair over. "Now, what has happened?"

I looked over at Cahal who began telling our uncle what he had seen earlier. I could see from my uncle's furrowed brows; the information took him by surprise. He said nothing while Cahal spoke and remained quiet when he was finished.

"We know there could be possible explanations to this that are not sinister, but you understand our hesitancy and indeed, our suspicions," I said.

Rexian nodded slowly. "Raeghar is a master of keeping his emotions in check. In many ways, Cahal you remind me of him. But this? I do not believe any malice was meant. Still, this is not something I can ignore. And if any ill is meant to Elyan, I would never forgive myself if something happened to him." Rexian stood and headed to the door. Opening it, he stopped when his eldest son appeared, poised to knock.

"Da'," Cinaeth said. "I just returned from patrol. I was going to see if you were still awake."

"Aye, lad, but I must see to something. Come with us? I believe you may need to be part of this."

Cinaeth nodded, his face still young for his nineteen years but his honey-colored eyes intense. I recognized my aunt's eyes and my heart hurt again for my uncle.

"Is there something wrong?" Cinaeth asked.

"Uncertain, we need to clear the air. Come," Rexian said.

We all followed the king down the hall to another room. Knocking loudly on the oak door, as we were all familiar with the sounds coming from behind the door, we waited. After a short pause, there was the sound of the bolt being slid back and the door opened to reveal Uncle Elyan, flushed and slightly out of breath, wearing only his trews.

"Brother?" He questioned moving the door so we could not see inside. If the situation were not so intense, I would have laughed. Both Cahal and I had experienced that sort of interruption with our father.

"Elyan, we need to speak with Connifarrah," Rexian said.

Elyan's nearly white eyes bounced from one to the other. "Right now?" He whined.

I did laugh at that but quickly sobered when Rexian looked back at me.

"Aye, now," Rexian stated then turned to Cinaeth. "Go to your Uncle Raeghar and have him join us." Cinaeth nodded and headed down the hallway. Turning back to Elyan, Rexian continued. "Five minutes. Dress and join us in my solar."

Elyan's shoulders fell but he nodded and slowly closed the door. Cinaeth soon returned with Raeghar and the same blonde warrior Cahal had seen before following.

"What is going on, Rexian?" He demanded. "I was in conference with Teren." He nodded toward the blonde male.

"Aye, and I am glad your lieutenant is with you," Rexian said. "Come with me." He turned to head up the stairs.

Once we were in his solar, it was quiet until Elyan and Connifarrah entered. She looked pale in her eyes flashed to Raeghar.

"You wanted to speak with me, your Majesty?" She asked.

Rexian heaved a sigh and turn to look at her. "What have been your movements this evening, Connifarrah?" He asked and again her eyes bounced to Raeghar's.

"This evening, sire?" She asked.

"Aye, after supper, what did you do?"

"Well, I... I retired, sire," she answered.

"And you have not left your room all evening?"

"I..."

"Rexian, I must ask," Elyan broke in. "What is this about?"

Rexian ignored him. "Did you leave your room at all this evening, Connifarrah?"

She swallowed hard and glanced again at Raeghar. "Of course she didn't," Elyan said.

"Really, Rexian that is enough," Raeghar stated.

The king's back bristled and he turned his stone-like dragon eyes to him. "And you? War Chief? What were your movements?" His voice was the rough sound of a dragon.

Raeghar snapped to attention and spoke low. "I was on patrol."

"Ehm, I'm sorry, Uncle," Cinaeth stepped forward. "I just returned from patrol. You were not there."

"You question your War Chief, boy?" The lieutenant, Teren stepped forward almost protective of Raeghar. My uncle placed his hand on Teren's arm. They locked eyes and Raeghar shook his head slightly but did not speak.

"And you will not forget your place, Lieutenant, nor to whom you speak. Remember your future king," Rexian spat.

"My apologies, sire, your majesty," Teren looked down and stepped back.

"You do not speak, Raeghar. You will say nothing? Give me one good reason I should not have you escorted from my sight right now. I need someone at my side I can trust."

"You can trust me," Raeghar interjected.

"You lied to me. How can you say that?" Rexian demanded. His eyes were back to his human form. "Where were you?"

Raeghar pulled himself up to his full height and raised his chin but did not speak. The brothers locked eyes but soon, Rexian sighed.

"Very well. You leave me no choice," Rexian turned to his son. "Cinaeth, escort your uncle to a cell in the dungeon until he is willing to speak to me."

"You dare lay a hand on him—" Teren stepped forward at the same time Connifarrah screeched "Nay!"

"Enough, both of you. Conni, say nothing," Raeghar ordered.

"My Lord, please! Raeghar is loyal to you! He—"

"Enough, Connie. Say no more."

"You know your brother, sire," Teren tried.

"Enough, Teren," he ordered. "You say nothing." The lieutenant locked eyes with Raeghar and pleaded with him.

"Farrah?" Elyan questioned looking at his mate. "My love, what is going on?"

Her eyes bounced to Raeghar until Elyan stood before her. She allowed a tear to slip down her cheek.

"It is my fault," she said.

"Nay, Conni," Raeghar replied.

"I will not have brother against brother. Not when I have a chance to explain," she stated.

I knew in that moment whatever their secret was, it was not malicious. Rexian motioned her forward.

"My Lord, I will have your promise. If what I tell you is acceptable and proves Raeghar did no wrong, you will let him be."

"Depending on what you tell me, I agree," Rexian stated.

"Very well," she straightened and glanced back at her mate. "I enlisted Raeghar's assistance. I needed to meet with someone and I did not wish to go alone."

"Farrah, why didn't you ask me?" Elyan questioned.

"I did not wish you to find out, Elyan. Raeghar agreed and he flew me too... Burren Woods in Korlon's land."

I tried to prevent my body from reacting and from how still Cahal went beside me he did too.

"Why in the name of the gods, would you want to go into

enemy territory?" Rexian demanded

"Because it was the only place Una would meet," she explained.

"Una? The witch?" Elyan challenged.

She nodded.

"Why, Connifarrah?" Rexian questioned. "Why did you want to meet with her?"

"I had to."

"Why?" Elyan pressed.

"Because I am aging," she blurted. "And soon I will not be able to give you the child I know you so desperately want. I am over forty years. I only have another year if that and I know how much you desire children."

The room went silent. "Farrah," Elyan finally started and reached for her. "You are who and what I want."

"I am older than you, Elyan. I will not be able to conceive much longer, and I will not condone you taking another to your bed to have a child. I cannae."

"What are you talking about? I am not nor will I ever take another to my bed."

"You want a child. You have always wanted a child and I may not be able to give you one," she did not try to wipe the tears that fell. Elyan enveloped her in an embrace.

"What does Una have to do with this?" Rexian asked. "And why didn't you clear this with me, Raeghar?"

"Una gave me a potion to take just before we…" Connifarrah trailed off.

Realization dawned on Elyan's face. "That is why you

were so adamant we make love this evening. Farrah, how many times do I have to tell you, you are enough for me. Always have been, always will be."

"For how long? Love will only take us so far. And I want to give you a child. I miss my child. My daughter's life was cut short, there will be nothing of me left in this world."

"Your daughter?" I asked.

"I am Farrah's second mate," Elyan explained quickly then turned back to her. "So long as we have each other, nothing else matters. No matter what. No more going off on your own. The gods only know what was in that potion." He looked up at his brother. "Raeghar, why? Why did you let her do this?"

"You try stopping your mate when she's put her mind to something. It's not easy. I only found out because I found her out by the woods speaking into a tree stump. She told me everything. I was going to come to you but…"

"I begged him not to," she said.

"What was the price for this?" Rexian asked.

"Fifty gold coins," Raeghar replied. "Which I took it from my share."

Rexian huffed. "Well, at least it wasn't the other thing we thought it could be."

"What other thing?" Elyan asked.

"The way it looked and sounded, we thought it could have been poison. We hoped it wasn't and are happy their plan wasn't to murder you," Rexian stated.

"Murder?" Connifarrah gasped. "Never."

"I swear on my life, brother, I would never be part of

that," Raeghar pledged.

"'Tis glad I am to hear that. Now, let us all get to bed and hear no more on this."

"Which one of you followed us?" Raeghar turned to Cahal and me.

Cahal step forward. "Me."

"Lemon water," Raeghar nodded, looking over at Teren. "I thought so. I looked when I heard flapping above me but could not see anything."

"As you know, my dragon his black and I have learned to blend in with the sky at night when needed."

"I'm sorry you thought we meant ill," he continued. "Looking back, I can see why."

"After our own experiences with familial betrayal, I'm afraid we are a little suspicious of everyone," I explained.

"With reason," Raeghar agreed.

Teren pursed his lips together. He clearly wasn't happy with our accusation.

"Let us all retire," Rexian stated. "There has been enough excitement for one night."

Once we were back in their rooms, Cahal turned to look at me.

"Korlon's land?"

"Aye, I heard it too. Something to speak to our uncle about tomorrow."

"It did not sound like they were friendly. And yet Korlon's mercenaries thought the dragon king was the one in league with him," Cahal said, then huffed. "What is going on here,

Finn?"

I shook my head. "I do not know, Cahal. But whatever it is we must be cautious. Our uncles will not appreciate more accusations."

"Agreed. Let's get some sleep, things tend to look better after a good night's rest."

"Aye, good night, brother."

After wishing each other a good sleep, we kept the adjoining door open and I crawled into bed. It was much colder without Brigid next to me and not being able to stroke her stomach, kissing my whelp within her made my hand itch and my heart clench. Reminding myself it was only for another night, two at most before I would hold her again, I shut my eyes and tried to sleep.

Chapter Five

Cahal

I left Finn in the Great Hall to break his fast. I never ate so early, and much preferred exercise in the morning. After telling him I would check in with Drake and our males on the mainland, I headed out to the steps, leading to the water.

Admittingly, a castle surrounded by water on all sides

was a good idea militaristically, but for someone who found water a necessary evil, I was not amused. Or rather my dragon was not happy. He would much prefer to shift on land and take to the sky than to dive and swim in water, unless we were taking a bath.

I had shucked my plaid but just as I was about to pull off my tunic, I heard a deep voice behind me speak, "going for a swim?"

Turning, I came face to face with my Uncle Raeghar.

"Exercise," I replied. "And to check on our males across the water."

My uncle slowly nodded. "Care for company?"

I watched him. He could have many reasons to ask to join me. But in a sign of good faith, I agreed and soon we were both in the water. The silver dragon glided along the surface like a swan. His silver brown eyes did not meet mine and soon we were near enough to the land to climb out. I was proud our males had seen us coming and prepared to defend the camp in case I needed assistance. Raeghar and I shifted, and I wrapped my plaid around my hips as my uncle tugged on his tunic.

"Anything to report?" I asked Drake, my brother's War Chief's lieutenant after introductions were made.

"All quiet here, sire," Drake stated. "How do you and our king fair?" His eyes darted to Raeghar, his distrust clear.

"We are well, I thank you for your concern and will be sure to tell our king of your diligence," I said, then continued. "My uncle and I are going on a quick flight. We will return."

"We will be watching for you." Drake's message was clear, they were there if I needed them.

"We will not be long," I said and soon my uncle and I were in the air flying over the woods and plains passing several human villages below. Some farmers stopped and waved at us. When I noticed a wall, Raeghar banked sharply to the right and I followed, intent on asking why he flew so fast away from the area.

We had flown together for an hour when he motioned with his back talon to find a place to land. After circling a grassy plain, Raeghar landed and shifted. I followed and my uncle waited until I wrapped my plaid around me to speak.

"Why'd you believe the worst of me when you saw what you saw?"

"Think how it looked, Uncle," I replied. "Secret looks between you two and you and Teren. Sneaking off into the dead of night with your brother's mate and buying a potion mixed with dragon blood from a witch? Then lying about it? What would it look like to you?"

He huffed and looked away. "I would have hoped my nephew, the lad I trained, would have spoken with me first."

"That lad is now a grown male and he is beholden to none but his king."

"Not even his own family?"

"Family betrayed me. Family killed. You speak of family and yet have no concept what Finn and I went through. What our mother, your sister went through. You have no place to ask that, Uncle. I sent you word when I was sure of Teyrnon's," I shook my head. "Of Nameless' motives and you never replied. So forgive me, if I do not believe in the family of which you speak.

"I received no message from you," he answered. "And as for familial betrayal, you cannot give a dead male that much power over you."

"Do you ken the pain that comes with seeing your youngest brother's throat being ripped out? Of seeing him fall to his death and knowing your other brother was the cause? And you could not get to him in time?"

Raeghar shook his head. "Nay, but I ken the pain of loss. And if I can help any of my sisters-by-mating especially, Farrah, then I will."

"Are you in love with her?"

He looked at me like I had grown another dragon head. "Conni? Nay, she is a friend. Besides, I am unable to marry as War Chief, so I do not love."

I read the truth in his eyes and conceded. "When Tahra was taken, and we learned those paid to steal her spoke of an alliance between the dragon king and another, we, all of us, worried it was Rexian."

"I can swear on my life, Rexian would and could never do as you say. He loves Tahra as his own daughter. We all do. She is special as she is the only blood female born in your generation." We paused for a long moment before he spoke again. "You asked a personal question of me which I answered truthfully. Now, I ask the same of you. What else are you not telling us?"

It was the moment of truth. Either I told him and lost our secret, or I did nae tell him and lose his assistance. I weighed my options carefully and decided.

"Korlon," I started. "They said the dragon king was in league with Korlon. That was who took Tahra and who would have forced her to mate him. The accomplice we spoke to, claimed the dragon king promised her to him."

"That's rubbish. One, Rexian is adamantly against arranged matings and two, Korlon is our enemy. His lands abut ours. We flew close today. He has killed dragons and his own people for sport."

"I wondered why you banked so quickly."

"He does not take kindly to dragons on his land. Now, I understand your suspicions. But why of me?"

"Before Nameless died, he made a bargain with the Lewis Laird. Kill Finn, blame me, then become king. He considered himself king. Could that sickness not be common enough among younger brothers?"

"Is it something you have?"

"Nay," I snapped. "I am loyal to my king."

"Then what makes you think I am any different?"

He was right of course. I had seen his loyalty to Rexian even against their father who would taunt Rexian saying Florian his favorite, and the second to the youngest was stronger and better suited to the temperament of kingship. What the old dragon meant was, Florian was just as cruel as he was. Rexian was fair.

"Then will you join us as we go to Korlon's land and speak with him? Spare some warriors?" I asked.

"We will speak with Rexian first," Raeghar replied. "Then aye, I have been waiting for a moment where I could pummel that sorry arse. He has many sins against his name, and I would be happy to play god to give him his well-earned comeuppance."

"You really donnae like him, Uncle," I chuckled.

"How could you tell?" He teased.

149

It felt good to banter with my uncle. It was rare that he would tease but when he did it was always fun. I had missed both he and Rexian when I left to go home from fostering. Rexian, though tough, was always there with an embrace and a "well done" after a tough day. Raeghar on the other hand, was much stricter and on the rare occasions I did hear "well done" from him, it meant more than all of Rexian's combined because I had truly earned it.

"Come now, let us return before your males send out a scouting party for you."

"They're loyal," I admitted.

"And very well trained," Raeghar said. "I am glad to see your training stuck with you. Though I am sure your father continued your teachings."

"He taught me to be a great warrior," I agreed. *"You* taught me to be a great War Chief."

Raeghar pulled himself up to his full height and puffed out his chest with the grin. "'Tis glad I am... You were a horrible listener."

I barked a laugh, and he slung his arm around my shoulders. "I can only apologize when I say I will never hold the same title as you, Uncle. I will never be War Chief."

"Nay, you are the king's most trusted advisor. That is important. I have one and so does Rexian. It is an honorable position."

"Teren," I offered.

"What about him?" Raeghar questioned.

"He is your most trusted advisor," I stated.

"He is."

"He's protective of you."

"Aye, and I of him. He's a great friend."

"You trust him?"

"With my life, and so much more."

"Good, then I would like to meet him properly."

"I can arrange that," Raeghar replied. "Let us go back, now." We walked through the woods content to speak of happier times. He was a listening ear and after we walked the long way back, our conversation turned to my recent mating. Though surprised, Raeghar listened and did not speak until the spires of the castle came into view above the tops of the trees.

"I cannot say I am surprised you stepped forward to marry the lass, you have the highest of valor, but I have to say what I am surprised with, Cahal is, that you stepped forward at all. Knowing the history between you two, and everything that happened with Bearcbhan and Sybine and you, I have to say, I am a wee bit surprised."

"If I am being truthful, Uncle, I am surprised as well. But she needed me."

"And, you have to admit, you could not think of her being mated to another."

"That is true. What do I do? She claims she wants to be with me, but whenever we are anywhere remotely near to that, she either clams up, cries her eyes out, or calls me by my dead brother's name. I'm under no delusion they were together, they have whelps for goodness' sake," I heaved a sigh. "But I was not expecting it to be so in my face, you ken? I donnae know what to do, Uncle."

"Though I am unmated," Raeghar began. "I do have some

experience with passion. I do not envy you, nephew. I truly do not envy you, but what I can say is... You went rogue and when you went rogue, you were the one, the Prince, the War Chief, the most trusted advisor, the second born of the king, *you* were the one who brought yourself back, not the dragon, not Finn, not your father, not your mother, not your love for Sybine, you, your strength. My point is, if you can fight a rogue dragon, the love of your life should not be that difficult, aye?"

I paused. "I had not thought of it like that."

"Truly, lad I am proud of you. Stepping forward the way you did. Taking their whelps under your house and providing for them. Work with her, not against what Bearcbhan was to her. Be yourself, be the male she fell in love with. Be the male she wanted. Only *you* can do that. Only *you* have the strength. And *only* you will know what to do."

We arrived at the camp and my warriors were alert, wary. But with a single nod, Drake stood down.

"Are you all well?" I asked unsure if they had enough food.

"Aye, my Lord," Drake answered. "We have food aplenty from the woods. We thank his majesty for replanting the trees."

"I will take your gratitude to my king," Raeghar said. "I am certain he will have you all dine with us on the final night you are here. But now, we go to break our fast."

My males bowed and we walked to the bank of the lough. Once in our dragon form, we flew back to the keep.

Finn

As I waited for Cahal to return, I spoke at length with Cinaeth, my eldest cousin. He found me at the dais, breaking my fast, and had many questions about the first few days of being king. Not that, at nineteen, he expected to be king yet, I still applauded his desire to learn. I saw much of my late aunt in him, and my heart hurt for both he and my uncle. I could not imagine having the burden of being king without my true mate by my side. And their sons, I shook my head, two were under the age of ten and though Cinaeth was the eldest, two more were only sixteen and fifteen, fostering with a dragon clan north in Norway. We had just finished talking when Cahal and Raeghar returned. Raeghar nodded to me and headed up the stairs toward the king's solar as Cahal walked over to the dais.

"Cinaeth," he greeted our cousin.

"Cahal," he smiled. "Congratulations on your mating. I overheard. That is delightful."

"Thank you," Cahal replied. "How is your search for a mate going?"

The younger man smiled salaciously. "Ah, come now, I am far too young to settle down." He chuckled. "I'm having too much fun." His brows bounced.

Cahal and I laughed. Not too long ago we thought the same. "Though I will say, I have met a female who has piqued my interest."

"Indeed? That is excellent."

"But I am not willing to speak of it yet," Cinaeth said.

"Understood."

Then, Cahal leaned forward. "Tell me, cousin, where

would one go if they had a taste for human females? Is there a local pub?"

Knowing Cahal would remain faithful to Sybine made me wonder what he was thinking. But I kept quiet.

"Ehm... Cahal, you were just mated," Cinaeth said.

"Not for me!" Cahal laughed. "Duncan asked."

Duncan, my healer's son and her assistant, had not shown an interest in a female since I could remember. My belief was, he was too shy, but you're a highly skilled warrior and healer, I had never found. Cahal was up to something.

"Oh! Forgive me," Cinaeth replied. "Well – ehm – there is a place near the border of our lands. I have heard the males speak of it."

"Ah, you've *heard*, aye?" Cahal winked.

The younger male beamed. "Perhaps I've done more than just heard."

"I would imagine so as the same blood flows in our veins," I winked. "Is it north?"

"Southwest," he confirmed.

"Good," Cahal said. "I will tell him."

"Tell who what?" Rexian's voice came beside the steps up to the dais.

"Da'!" Cinaeth jumped then sent a pleading look to us.

"I was asking Cinaeth about the closest human village," I stated.

"More the pub if I overheard correctly," our uncle winked. "Though I am glad it was not for yourselves or I would need to teach you a lesson in respecting your mates, king or no king," he teased.

"Believe me, Uncle, Brigid is the only one for me. I love her more than life itself," I stated.

A gasp echoed across the seemingly empty Great Hall. Our eyes turned to see Connifarrah and Elyan standing at the base of the stairs. We all stood in greeting. Pale and shaking, Farrah gripped her mate's hand as he walked her over to us.

"Sister, are you well?" Rexian asked.

She swallowed audibly, but her eyes never left mine. "Brigid?" She questioned.

"Aye, my lady, my wife and true mate, Queen Brigid McKay."

"Lewis?" She asked.

"Aye, her maiden name was Lewis but has not been for many months. Do you ken her? For certs, she would be glad. Her parents were killed, and she lived a lonely life before she came to us."

"How..." She breathed, then, leaned into Elyan. "How did her parents die?"

Her father was War Chief, it was in battle when she was very young... Her mother... It does not bear repeating, my lady."

"Tell me," she snapped.

My eyes widened at her vehemence.

"Shh, shh," Elyan soothed her.

"Her mother was accused of being a witch and burned at the stake. My mate was thirteen. She was alone ever since. And a stronger, more beautiful lass you'll never meet," I said. Just thinking of her make my chest ache.

Connifarrah's breathing increased and she licked her lips as if they were dry. "What age is she?"

"She just turned twenty-one."

Connifarrah stared at me, then her eyes rolled back and she fainted into Elyan.

Chapter Six

Cahal

"Sarrah," Elyan cried as she fell into him. "Call for the healer."

"She's delivering whelps on the other side of the territory," Rexian jumped in as he trotted down the steps, hurrying toward her. Raeghar helped Elyan get ahold of her and lifted her into her mate's arms.

Finn looked at me. "Duncan," he said but I was already racing to the door. Shouting across the way, Duncan shifted and flew as fast as he could. As he shifted back, hurrying into the Great Hall, I explained the lady had just fainted. Duncan grabbed his pouch from his ankle and found a small glass bottle, uncorking it, he waved it under her nose. The smell caused all the dragons to go dizzy but Connifarrah woke with a start.

"Elyan," she cried.

"I'm here, my love," he said softly. "Are you all right?" He turned her gently toward him.

"Aye," pressing the heel of her hand to her forehead, she groaned. "My head, it hurts."

"It will for a short time, my lady," Duncan said, then poured some hot water over some herbs crushed in a cup. Swirling it around I caught the smell of willow bark and lavender. "Drink this slowly, it will help."

She took the cup with both hands and sipped. Uncle Elyan had not moved from her side. Raeghar paced behind the chair where he had helped his brother carry her.

"I am well, forgive me," she first looked to Elyan then to Raeghar.

"Do not apologize, Farrah," Rexian said. "We want to be sure you are well."

"I am. Thank you, my king," she answered then looked up at Finn. "Forgive me, my lord but your news was shocking."

"I am very sorry, my lady," Finn bowed to her.

"Nay, no need," she answered then looked to her mate. "Do you think it could be?"

"I do not see how, my love," Elyan shook his head. "You remember what he said. She drowned."

"He said I was burned at the stake when I was in prison until you rescued me. Could he not have lied about this as well?"

"You rescued yourself, my love. I just happened to be there."

"Oh dear gods, my baby. She lived so long without anyone."

"Forgive me," Finn step forward. "Could you please explain what is going on?"

She looked at Elyan then back at Finn. "Before I do, my lord, forgive me, but does your mate have red hair?"

"Aye," he answered cautiously. "And the deepest blue eyes I have ever seen."

She moaned and rolled her head to rest on her husband's shoulder. "It cannot be," Elyan said.

"What can't be?" Finn demanded.

Connifarrah looked over at my brother and took a deep breath.

"My name is not Connifarrah from birth, rather it was the name given and chosen for me when I arrived here. Elyan has already explained he found me in a glen surrounded by conifers and injured," she motioned to the scar on her face. "I am sure your healer will explain how this sort of injury would affect my memory."

We looked at Duncan for confirmation. He nodded, "I have done some study on it, my king."

"Well, when I came to my senses, I did not remember my

name nor anything about my history. It came back slowly over time in the form of dreams. I would wake screaming something about Brochan. Elyan was so good as to stay with me on the maids pallet in my room. I felt safe knowing he was there. He would help me and in that time between sleep and waking he was able to ask me questions about my life. I had been married to a man; Brochan who had died in battle. He was War Chief." She glanced up at Raeghar who smiled softly encouraging her to continue.

"After he died, I was unable to save the life of the laird's wife and she died in childbirth. He had me arrested and thrown in the dungeon where I remained for five years until I was able to escape. When I did, I tried to run back to my cottage on the outskirts of a wood to my daughter. But I was followed, pursued by the laird's men and dogs. I got away but tripped over my own feet and fell, striking my head on a rock. I donnae ken what happened after that, until Elyan found me When I finally remembered that I had a daughter, we hurried back to Lewis' land to find her but when we found the cottage, it was empty. No one had lived there for many months and when we went to the laird for explanation, he told us my daughter, my Brigid was dead. Drowned in the sea. We came back here, and I mourned her. But now, if what you say is correct..."

"How long ago did you go to the laird?" Finn's voice was tight.

"We went in the spring, Finn," Elian said.

"Brigid and I were mated mere weeks before Yuletide," Finn answered. "The cottage would have been empty five months."

"She's alive," she stated then looked at Elyan with pleading eyes. "That bastard lied to me!"

"I will kill him," Elyan growled his eyes flashing to dragon slits.

"Too late, Uncle," Finn stated. "I avenged my mate by killing her tormentor four months ago."

"Tormentor?" Farrah shrieked. "Dear gods, what did he do to her?"

"She lived in fear for years thinking the same fate of her mother would befall her. Why did everyone think you were burned?"

Her hand went up to the stippling of flesh on her neck. "There was much he did to torture me. I am certain he spread the rumor of my death just as he spread Brigid's. Where is she? How is she? Can I see her?"

Finn held up his hands. "My lady, my mate is six months into carrying my heir, a shock like this will surely not be good for her nor our whelp. In good conscience, I cannae allow it."

"I have not seen my daughter in over seven years. I will not wait another second."

"Farrah," Elyan cautioned. "You would feel the same."

"My daughter has a will of fire just like her father. She is stronger than you think."

"I do not doubt her strength, only her safety. I will not lose her nor my child," Finn said.

"Excuse me," Rexian said softly, his voice cracking slightly as he turned and left the room.

"Da'?" Cinaeth questioned. Rexian waved but did not turn around. "I'll go see to him."

Watching my cousin leave the room to check on his

father, I looked back at Finn.

"May I speak with you, brother?"

Finn nodded once and we walked over to the hidden door Connifarrah used the first time we met her. Once the door was shut, we were in complete darkness, but our dragon sight was keen.

"As much as I am pleased for Brigid and you, your mate has a right to know her mother is alive. Think if the positions were switched. Would you not want to know too?" I asked.

"I am not denying it, but I am not six months into carrying a whelp. Duncan and his mother told me if Brigid has a shock she could lose him."

"You put too much stock in believing them, brother. And not enough in your mate. Connifarrah is right. I have seen it, as you have. Brigid has a will as strong as dragon fire. But I digress. Finn, we need to stay on point here. I know this news is sudden and needs attention, but so does the reason we are here. Korlon. We need to plan."

Finn nodded. "You always do keep me honest, brother. I thank you. Let us return. Ask for our uncle to come back and see if we can come up with a plan."

"I do have one... Well, a formation of one."

"I am interested in hearing it. Come now, thank you for keeping me honest and focused."

"I believe we both have reasons to hurry this meeting along and get home."

"Aye, we do," Finn agreed. "Come then, brother let us go talk to our uncles."

As soon as we entered the Great Hall, Rexian came into

view. His eldest son beside him.

"Forgive me for leaving so abruptly earlier," Rexian began, his eyes strained. "I had something that needed my attention."

Instead of embarrassing him by bringing up the fact we all smelled a lie and the pain he was experiencing when Finn mentioned losing Brigid and their whelp, we sat and continued our discussion.

"As much as I am glad to know my mate's mother is alive, I will be cautious," Finn concluded talks of Brigid. "Now, if we may get back to Korlon."

"What about him? He's a spoiled brat who needs to be taught a lesson," Raeghar stated.

"Indeed," Finn answered. "And that is what I'm hoping will happen. Cahal? Your plan?"

"Uncle Raeghar told me of Korlon and where his lands were. My thought is this, send him word that the princess has been taken and will be delivered to him but the price has doubled because Arnol is dead."

At my uncles' and cousin's confused faces, Finn explained. "Arnol was the leader of the group who abducted Tahra."

I continued. "So have one of us pose as the one negotiating, to bring him out. He is human, he will not be able to smell the dragon born on us. Say, I meet him. We will find out who is claiming to be the dragon king and who gave Tahra to him."

"I am pleased she is safely away from that creature," Rexian said. "We may be able to shift into serpents, but he is the son of the devil. God help any in his clutches."

"Agreed. Do any of you know him on sight? And, more importantly, does he know any of you?" Cahal asked.

"He knows me," Rexian said. "I visited him when he took over for his father."

"Aye and unfortunately, he knows me too," Raeghar replied.

"I've never met him," Elyan stated.

"I know him." We look toward Cinaeth. "I mean… Well, I have seen him. I was part of the warriors who protected you da'. I was in the sky when you met him. I know what he looks like. I could identify him."

"Are you sure? Males look different from the sky," Raeghar said.

I could tell Rexian wanted to defend his son as prince, but he paused. It was a test. Raeghar was always teaching the younger generation. After fostering there as a lad, I knew his tests well. The young man straightened and locked eyes with his uncle.

"Aye, I am certain," Cinaeth said.

"Good," Raeghar replied.

I held in my grin. Many a time did I experience Raeghar's assessments. I was proud of my cousin. He passed.

"Then, we send a message tonight," Finn stated and turned to Rexian. "Uncle, may I borrow some parchment?"

Duncan leaned over to me. "May I speak, my lord?"

"Of course," I answered him, then spoke louder. "Finn, Duncan has asked to speak."

"Speak, friend, we stand on no ceremony here," Finn

encouraged.

"Forgive me, my king. But might I suggest, royal parchment would be too clean for a mercenary. The man may not be intelligent to raid our castle and steal her highness, but surely he would see the trickery in a pristine piece of parchment."

"Wise words," Finn agreed. "Some butcher's paper, perhaps?"

"Aye," Duncan agreed. "And I would be happy to write it for you, my king. Your elegant hand would be recognizable as a learned male."

"Thank you, Duncan, aye," Finn replied. "Let's go now and get the message out. Do you think you could find someone to take the message to him?"

"Aye," Raeghar replied looking over at his lieutenant, who nodded. "Teren knows some human men who would do just about anything for coin."

"Take some from the treasury this time," Rexian approved, then we four headed to the kitchen as Raeghar and Teren walked out the backdoor with Cinaeth in tow.

Cahal

The message was written and Duncan's crude hand and handed to Teren. As soon as our uncle's lieutenant left to deliver it, Finn and I took a moment alone in our chambers. My brother heaved a long-suffering sigh and flopped down in the chair by the window.

"What on earth am I going to tell Brigid?" he questioned.

"What do you mean?" I asked.

"Her mother? Here? Alive? After all this time?" He got to his feet and walked to the window, gazing out across the lough toward our males' encampment. Some dragons flew high above, while others sat around the fire. He was silent for a long moment and I went to the decanter. Pouring two large glasses of whiskey, I approached him. Though he didn't turn to me, I offered the glass and looked out the window beside him.

Comfortable silence engulfed us and soon, I felt a sort of peace and familiarity descend. I didn't realize how much I had missed him until that moment. We still said nothing but watched another of our team shift and take to the sky.

"What we must look like to the outside world," Finn said softly

I shrugged. "Not sure I ever really thought about it," I said taking sip of whiskey.

Finn was quiet again. I didn't push, he needed time to wrap his head around everything. He was crowned king, our sister was kidnapped, he journeyed on his first diplomatic mission, and found his mate's mother who had been presumed dead, all within days.

"I am glad you were here, Cahal," he said. "I'm glad to have you by my side again."

"I am glad to be here," I answered.

Finn breathed deeply and turned to me. "So," he said after taking a long drink. "Tell me more about this plan of yours."

Chapter Seven

I took a sip of my watered-down ale and looked around the pub. The place was one of the dirtiest places I had ever seen and that meant something as I had been to some squalid places.

Cinaeth sat on one of the stools, an eye on me. Uncle

Raeghar had heard from Teren that the note was delivered so, I waited.

Finn and our uncles crouched in the darkness just outside the door, close enough to hear with their dragon hearing.

Another sip of ale and I looked up to see the door open. I had hunched my large frame to look smaller, as most human men were not as large as dragons. But when the male at the door looked around the pub, his body was tense. Glancing at my cousin, Cinaeth's brows furrowed but he did nae look my way. Instead, he kept his gaze locked on the newcomer.

When the male, I had yet to catch his scent to say if he were human or dragon, saw him, he walked over. Leaning against the counter, he spoke low. Too low. All I could see was my cousin's face. His eyes widened as he listened, then glanced at me.

Something was wrong.

Cinaeth stood so fast the stool was thrown across the room. A hush descended and his breathing picked up. I also heard the pitter patter of his heart racing.

Something was very wrong.

With a quick glance at me, he threw some coins on the counter to pay and raced out of the room, followed closely by the male. The door opened and a gust of wind blew both of their scent toward me. Dragon, clearly my cousin Cinaeth's scent. The other was human and dragon and... kin.

I smelled my mother's family's blood. Every instinct made me want to jump up and race after them, but I suppressed it. I had a duty. Finn could take care of it. He did not need me. And yet... I strained to hear any conversation outside but all I could hear over the din of bawdy conversation around me, was the whoosh of dragons taking flight.

Something was horribly wrong.

Finn

I saw the young warrior enter the pub but I did not know him. Raeghar was beside me and I felt him tense.

"What is it?" I questioned.

"The lad…" He began. "He is Talisian's son."

"Uncle Talisian?" I asked. I had not seen my third born uncle in years.

"Aye, he left when Father would not agree to his mating a human. A human from Korlon's clan. The lad fostered with me once Rexian took over. What is he doing here?"

"Let's find out." I was about to enter the pub when Cinaeth race out, followed closely by the male I saw enter.

"Uncle," Cinaeth said. "He refused. He marches on Lough Leane."

"Ooh that bastard," Raeghar breathed.

"He knows," I stated.

We looked at Talisian's son, who nodded.

"Mother overheard talk among the ladies. Korlon expected his bride yesterday. When he received the note, he went into a rage and swore vengeance on the dragons. I don't think he knew it was you who sent the message though."

"I need to return to Lough Leane," Raeghar said. "Do you

know which way they're planning on attacking?"

"They come from the south through the woods," he revealed.

Raeghar looked at me. "Your warriors are our first line of defense."

"And there are none better," I replied. "Go, Uncle. I will get Cahal. We will see you soon." I took his arm in a warrior shake and watched as all three shifted into dragon form and flew away. Hurrying to the door, it opened before I had a chance and Cahal stood before me.

"What is going on?" He demanded.

"Korlon is marching on Lough Leane," I answered simply.

His eyes widened but he nodded once and we hurried further away under the cover of darkness to shift and fly.

Cahal and I flew fast, following our uncle and cousins. Soon the spires of Castle Lough Leane come into view above the tree line and with it, the sound of men shouting and dragon roars. I saw Drake's red dragon dive, grab a male in his talons, and drop him into the lough.

Raeghar flew circles around the castle along with two other dragons who I did not recognize and Rexian, his muddy red clay colored dragon flew midway between the land and the castle clearly itching to join the fight. Every time he got close, Raeghar would roar at him and he would have to retreat. As king, I understood the need for protection, but as a warrior, I kenned the passion to fight.

The humans numbered well into the hundreds but with our males numbering dozens and being dragons we could easily take the human army.

Looking over at my brother, I clenched my forearm talon and then motioned to our uncles. Cahal nodded and we flew toward the king and War Chief. Seeing the other dragons up close, I recognized Elyan's but not the golden one. My only thought was it was Teren. Cinaeth was commanding his males flying to cut off the human's escape.

A soft roar and I turned to my brother, he wanted to join in. I nodded once. He flew into the fray and the four dragons, Rexian, Raeghar, Elyan, and myself landed and shifted quickly. Teren still flying high above us.

"Apologies for our late arrival, Uncle," I teased.

"Nay, not to worry. Talisian came to tell us first then we sent Daighre to the village to get you. We had fair warning," Rexian stated.

"Daighre?" I asked.

"Aye, Talisian's son. Father banished him when he fell in love with a human." Rexian nodded up to one of the dragons. I said no more, it mattered little now with the battle looming before us.

I watched as Cahal swooped high into the air, a gathering signal and our warriors rallied and flew up behind him, flanking him. In a formation that resembled a V, they dived as one, Cahal at the front. The rainbow of colors of the dragons' fires lit the sky but then, I heard a roar.

My eyes snapped up to see Cahal bank past some trees, but his wings faltered. My stomach dropped seeing the spear sticking out from under Cahal's arm, the tender area was our one and only vulnerable place. Duncan, our healer flew toward him but Cahal's massive size faltered again.

"Cahal!" I bellowed. Without any thought apart from

saving my brother, I shifted and leapt into the air. Pushing my dragon harder than ever before, my eyes stayed locked on my brother who had enough fight in him to know to bank toward the water. His landing would be wet, but he wouldn't hurt himself further.

Grateful to have my cousin take over, I paid little heed to the battle around me. My one goal was to save my brother. For a horrifying moment, I saw Bearcbhan again and the helplessness I felt at seeing him die engulfed me. My dragon shook its head violently trying to rid our mind of the image and pushed us faster.

Cahal was closer than before. Duncan was on his heels. When I was close enough, I stopped, hovering over the trees, wings outstretched. The pain in Cahal's eyes worried me and I watched as he slowly gave in to the darkness. His eyes closed just as he barreled into me. Wrapping him in my wings, I allowed his momentum to spiral us toward the water. We landed with a splash. Sacrificing my wing hold on him, I held him in my arms and propelled us to the surface. He had pulled the spear out earlier, but I smelled the blood and my dragon roared. Breaking through the water, Duncan and Raeghar helped me pull him up. Rexian was shouting orders to the servants to get linens, hot water, and the healer. He joined the others to help heave Cahal's unconscious form up the water stairs.

"We have our healer getting ready. I know you have yours too," Rexian said with a glance at Duncan. "The battle is ours. He will be all right, lad."

His words of encouragement did not shake the feeling that I might be losing my only remaining brother.

A few others hurried toward us with a large cloth with rings at the four corners. With great effort, and under the watchful eye of Duncan, we rolled Cahal's unconscious dragon form onto the cloth and once he was secure, they fed a thick rope through the rings and Raeghar headed into the water to shift. Being the largest dragon, he easily picked Cahal up and carried him to the balcony three stories above us for the healers.

Duncan flew up with Raeghar and the rest of us raced up the stairs pulling on tunics as we went. As soon as we entered the room, I could smell it.

Dragon bane.

Duncan's face was grim as he leaned over my brother's prone form. My uncle's healer was stirring something foul smelling over the fire.

"How is he?" Rexian demanded.

"Life still beats within him," Raeghar appeared at our right having pulled on his tunic.

"I will not lie, my king," Duncan said to me. "The wound is deep and close to his heart. Add in the dragon bane..." Duncan shook his head.

My body tingled and my dragon roared for retribution. Clenching my fist, I looked up at Duncan.

"Do what you can to save my brother," I told him. He bowed and I refused to see the skepticism in his eyes. "Did you see who threw the spear?"

"I did not. I am sorry, sire," he replied.

I thanked him and turned to the door. Leaving the room was difficult but I was alone in the hallway and the fear fell over me like a blanket. I could not lose my brother.

My breathing increased and my eyes flashed back and forth to my dragon slits. I was drowning and I could not break free. Seeing Cahal injured brought back the pain of seeing Nameless tear into Bearcbhan's neck, seeing my brother fall from the sky. Dead. The fear of losing Brigid and my child, the overpowering fear of hurting my dragons, being king. Everything came crashing down.

A hand landed on my shoulder and turned me around, pulling me into another room. Then, strong arms wrapped around me as the torrent released and I screamed into the shoulder of my Uncle Rexian as tears gushed from my eyes.

Not very kingly, I admitted, but I could nae help it. Rexian held me close until I got control. My dragon hid in the back of my mind, his strength giving me strength.

Finally, I pulled away from my uncle and wiped a hand down my face.

"Ugh," I moaned. "I apologize, Uncle." I stepped away and turned so he did not see me.

"Nay, do not apologize. I have been there. I know what it is you are feeling."

"Seeing him like that, I..."

"You remembered Bearcbhan and worried you might lose Cahal too. Then, the fear took hold. Fear of losing Brigid, fear of being king, and not knowing you feel ready. Fear that this battle may not end with a victory for us, though it is, and not knowing what will happen to us or your clan... Am I near enough the mark?"

I breathed a laugh and turned to look at him. "Aye, close enough, Uncle. You do know what I'm feeling."

"Because I have been there, lad. If it weren't for Raeghar and Elyan..." He shook his head as a look entered his eyes I could not discern. "They saw me at my lowest when Niamh died. I would not be here without them. Father and Velkin marched on us during that time. I was willing to give it all up, but they brought me back and I fought."

"March? What do you mean?" I asked.

"My father tried to regain his throne and convinced my brother to join him. Niamh had just died, and I was shattered. But they helped me back from the abyss. You have me. Cahal will be well but never fear sharing how you truly feel with me. Truthfully, lad, you will have no judgment from me."

I nodded. "Thank you, Uncle."

Rexian embraced me once more and we broke apart at the knock on the door. When my uncle opened it, Teren and Cinaeth stood smiling on the other side.

"Thank the gods," Rexian breathed and cupped his son's face then took Teren's arm in a shake. "We are victorious?"

"We are," Cinaeth grinned.

"Casualties?"

"Many on their side, my king. Minor flesh wounds on ours," Teren said.

"Raeghar will be pleased you are well, Teren. I know he cares a good deal for you."

"It is mutual, sire," Teren smiled. "He is a good leader."

"Aye, he is that," Rexian agreed.

Cinaeth stepped forward. "How is Cahal?"

"Our healers with him," I announced.

"He is alive?" Teren questioned. "It seemed a nasty hit. I took care of the human who threw the spear, my lord."

"My thanks, Teren," I said. "Cahal is resting."

Raeghar entered just a moment later, locked eyes with Teren, and nodded his head but the shadows in his eyes lifted. "What is the report?"

"They retreated, War Chief. But we captured the leader. Korlon is in our dungeon," Teren explained.

"Excellent," Raeghar smiled at him. I had never seen my uncle smile. I stared for a long moment. Then, Rexian turned to me.

"Do you wish to do the honors? It might help you," Rexian offered.

I chuckled at my uncle's suggestion. But truthfully a little interrogation sounded... good.

Chapter Eight

We were escorted down to the dungeons by one of my uncle's warriors but even if I could not hear the sniveling arrogant weasel, I would have been able to find him.

"Do you know who I am? I will have your head for this!" He shouted in the dimly lit cavern. "Do not touch me, serpent. I command the mightiest army in Ireland. I will kill you!"

"That mighty army is no more," Uncle Rexian stated as he ducked to enter the cell. I followed and finally saw the male who tried to have my sister kidnapped. I couldn't help but laugh. Tahra would have been able to snap him like a twig.

"The king," the puny human sneered. "I'm honored. Welcome to my humble lodgings."

"Stop with the shite, Korlon," Rexian said. "This is King Aodhfionn MacKay, King of the Dragons on Skye and Laird of the MacKay and Lewis clans, brother to Tahra MacKay. He has some questions for you."

"If you want to know where your sister is, you're too late. I received a message from one of the men I hired. It is probably too late for you to find him at the pub and if I didn't show, he'd kill her. She wasn't worth as much as he was demanding but this," he looked around him as if saying the keep. "This is worth a pretty amount. There's always some other wench for me to marry."

My blood boiled. He had no respect for my sister and nearly cost my brother's life. But I had to remain calm.

"So you admit to stealing the princess away," I questioned.

"There was no stealing involved."

"Indeed? How do you reckon?" I asked.

"Is it stealing for a man to take his own wife from the family who denies her will?" Korlon stated the question.

I shook my head quickly, trying to clear it from the nonsense he just said.

"What are you talking about?" Rexian asked.

"The dragon king and I negotiated our union. He thought it would strengthen both of our clans. And when I saw the lass a year ago... Well, she was everything I dreamed of when I thought of a wife. Her body was made for my hands."

I could handle insults being hurled but the moment he crossed the line and began speaking of my sister in a manner unfit for any female, my restraint broke and I threw my fist into his jaw hardly satisfied when I heard the crunch of bone and teeth. Rexian placed a hand on my shoulder as I stared down at the human sprawled on the floor, spitting out what teeth he had left. Whirling around to face my uncle, the dragon king, I shook off his hand.

"You lied to me," I demanded.

"Never," he swore.

"Swear on something worthy, you did not sell my sister to this man."

Rexian squared his shoulders and looked me straight in the eye. "I swear on the soul of my true mate and unborn whelp, that I did not negotiate, nor order negotiations with this man for Tahra's hand. I never could."

"Exactly," the male grunted as he pulled himself up. "You're weak, Rexian. You do not deserve to be king. You do not even consider *yourself* a king. That is why the true king spoke to me and if all is going as expected, he marches on your keep right... now."

A loud roar overhead followed by a bang and rattle of stone shook our bodies.

"What in the name of the gods?" Rexian demanded.

Korlon smiled blood seeping out of his mouth. "The real dragon king is taking his throne back. You've become weak. And lead your people with a passive hand, not an iron fist that they deserve. You allow folly without retribution, and you've given positions of power to lowlifes and peasants. You've traded your father's golden throne for one of wood and you expect things to just continue? You had a chance to make your clan stronger than ever but you refused my offer, so I went to the one who was as angry as I. The one whose legacy you destroyed."

Rexian shook with anger.

"That's right, laddie, da' is coming back and he's not happy with you."

My uncle growled and turned on his heels, racing up the stone steps and out the dungeon. I followed as fast as I could.

As soon as I was free of the dungeon, I nearly collided with my uncle who stared up in the sky and the dragons flying around, dropping boulders.

"Bastard!" Rexian shouted at one particular dragon flying higher than the others.

Raeghar appeared in the doorway of the keep followed by Teren. Their eyes searched the skies as they hurried over to us.

"What in the—"

"Our father," Rexian spat. "And our brother."

"Velkin, the devil," Raeghar breathed. "Dragons! Attack formations!"

"But Chief!" One of the dragons yelled. "It is our own! I recognize my brother."

Raeghar whipped around and penned a man with a glare but he did not get a moment before Teren raced to the man and held him by the neck.

"You do as your War Chief instructed," Teren said. "Stand under one of those boulders, Silmian and then tell me how they are our own! If you do not fight for Raeghar and Rexian, you fight for Velkin and a male who kept you in servitude. Is that where your loyalties lie?"

"N-nay," the male stuttered.

"Then gather the dragons. We end this. Your brother chose his fate," Raeghar replied then turned back to look at his brother as I stood beside him.

"Get you both inside. I cannot have either of you injured," Raeghar ordered. "Since Cahal is not here right now, I ken that is what he would want, Finn."

"We fight, brother as we always do... together," Rexian stated.

"As family," I replied.

"As family," Raeghar replied then, his eyes drifted over the Teren.

"As family," Teren shrugged with a grin and a wink.

"Rexian! Raeghar! What's happening?" Elyan demanded racing over to us.

"We are at war, brother," Raeghar said. "Do you fight?"

"Are you serious?" Elyan questioned, his eyes flashing to slits. "Always," his rough dragon voice said.

"Good," Rexian replied then his eyes turned to dragon slits. "Let's finish this." We all stood beside him staring up at the dragons above us.

"What is our plan?" I asked.

"I have an idea," Rexian said.

Chapter Nine

Cahal

I stood on the banks of the loch that fed the ocean just outside our keep on Skye. The sun shone down on me, the warm summer day relaxing in only the way a lazy day could. Taking a deep breath of the warm air, I closed my eyes to savor the moment.

Once I opened my eyes, I looked around the bank to see a figure standing just at the edge of the water. The figure was one I knew well. Breathing a gasp as I recognized him, I walked over hesitantly.

"Bearcbhan?" I questioned when I stood beside him.

He turned his head to look at me and smiled. "Heya, Cahal."

"What? How? I mean… Am I dead?"

Bearcbhan chuckled. "Do you wish to be?"

"Nay!" I answered quickly. "I cannot leave Sy—." I paused.

"Sybine?" He completed for me, then gazed back over the loch. "You are not dead, brother. Though the veil between life and death is thin for you right now. I am able to speak with you." He turned from the loch and stood before me. "I'm glad it was you who stepped forward to mate with Sybine. I would have wished for no other male."

"It was my honor. You ken I've always loved her."

"Aye, of course, but you also respect her."

"It was something I failed to do in the past but will never forget to do now."

"I am glad," he said. It was so surreal speaking to my dead brother. I took a moment to take his elbow and pull him into an embrace.

"I am so sorry," I muttered into his hair.

"For what?" he questioned.

"For not getting to you in time," I admitted. "I knew it was Teyrnon, but I could not stop you. It should have been me."

"Nay, I was foolish," he replied. "I went without thinking." He pulled back just as a loud boom echoed across the loch. "My lads' dragons?"

"They are fine. Shifted just the other day."

"Thank the gods."

"They've asked for you. Sybine has tried to tell them, but they do not understand."

He nodded slowly. "I used to entertain them every morning so Sybine could rest. I miss them horribly. And my daughter. She is so beautiful. I miss rocking her to sleep."

"She will know you. All your children will know you as their father and me as their uncle. I will never take your place."

"Thank you," Bearcbhan said.

Another loud boom echoed across the water. I looked to see if I could tell what was causing the noise.

"Our uncle's castle is under attack," Bearcbhan said simply. "You are in danger. You must shift to human form. You will need to be small to escape."

"Attack? By whom?"

"Aye. You are wounded. Duncan is with you. Be careful," he said.

"How do I shift? Wake up?"

"Easy," his eyes turned to the water. "Get into the water." I looked at my youngest brother. "But do me one small favor before you go?"

"Anything."

"Tell Sybine I love her. And tell my whelps..." He broke off and looked down. "Tell my lads, I'll always be there for him.

To listen for me when they need me, I'll be there."

"You have my oath, Bearcbhan," I swore.

Another loud boom.

"You need to go now," he said. "Tell them all I love them. Mama, Tahra, Da', Finn."

"I will. We all miss and love you."

"I know. Take Sybine as your true mate, Cahal. You have my blessing to be with her which is more than I asked of you when I took her."

"She was not mine."

"She was, and I would be lying if I didn't find some sort of satisfaction being the first to mate. But she was always yours. I should never have interfered."

"You gave her a name when I was unable to. She told me about... why you mated. You are a noble and admirable dragon. I am honored to be your brother."

"As I am to be yours," Bearcbhan moved behind me. I turned to face him, my back to the loch.

"Now, it's time to say goodbye. Wake up, Cahal. Wake up." He pushed me hard and my heels caught a rock. I flailed out but soon felt the icy water hit my back and encompass me. My eyes still open, I saw the blurry figure of my youngest brother still on the banks. But I heard his voice as if he was next to me.

"Take care of her. I love you, brother."

My eyes shot open as another boom echoed across the keep. I felt the rattle to my very bones and groaned.

"Cahal?" I heard the panic in Duncan's voice.

Looking over at him, I watched as he backed up to the wall, his eyes wide.

"What's going on?" I demanded.

He didn't speak. Something must be happening for Duncan to be scared dumb... Then I looked out the window to see a boulder being dropped and another hurled at the keep. I dove for cover when it struck the side near my window. The stone splintered and large chunks sprayed the room.

Duncan shouted at me but when I looked up, he was pinned under a large piece of stone. And he was in pain.

"Duncan!" I shouted over the ringing in my ears. "I'm here, I'm coming."

One glance at the now much larger gaping hole in the wall to make sure nothing else was going to be slung our way, I raced to my healer.

Duncan was shouting in pain and each cry made me angrier at whoever attacked us. Hurrying to his side, he looked up at me and through the pain I saw fear.

"I'm not going to hurt you," I said. I was not sure why I said it but it seemed to be the thing he was most interested in.

He paused a second, still holding my gaze. I wasn't sure when in the chaos I realized my dragon was still in charge, but with the extra strength I felt and Duncan's fear, it was an easy leap to make.

After a moment, Duncan nodded and I took a deep breath.

Dragon, please help me save him and help me know what is going on.

You have my word. My beast answered me in our mind.

Nodding at hearing or rather feeling my dragon's pledge, I watched as scales appeared on my arms and my hand turned to dragon talons.

Duncan's breathing and heart rate accelerated.

"You have nothing to fear, healer," I said as I took hold of the boulder crushing his legs. "This will hurt."

Duncan nodded, reaching for his belt and biting into the leather. I locked eyes with him and at his nod, I lifted. He screamed around the belt. His legs shattered by the rock. Fortunately our advanced healing would help him but, I knew the pain would ease in an hour or so. But bones took longer to knit than cuts to close. Though the pain would ease, he would not have use of his legs for a week.

Another boulder was loosed and the crash rattled the castle. Duncan groaned and spat out the leather.

"Go," he shouted through clenched teeth.

"I will not leave you here."

"You must, Dragon. Finn needs you."

Another boom.

"I will not leave you here," my dragon swore.

Duncan flinched but nodded. As quickly as I could and blocking out Duncan screams of pain, my scales and talons retreated as I picked him up and slung him over my shoulder. I raced from the room, frantically looking around to find a safe place. I saw people running down the hall, some screamed, some carried linens and buckets while others were maneuvering whelps into the queen's solar with a secret tunnel.

"I need assistance!" I bellowed. Several dragon stopped and one female beckoned me into another room. "His legs. Is it safe here?"

"Aye, my lord," she replied. "As safe as it can be. It's an internal room where we bring whelps sometimes. They are with our lady in the Queen's solar."

I imagined their lady was Connifarrah. I nodded and laid Duncan on the small bed. He groaned softly, his brow was sweaty.

"His legs were crushed by a boulder," I explained as the female poured some water into the basin and wet a piece of linen.

"Oh gods, leave him with me, my lord. Your healer will be fine. I will watch over him." She soothed his brow with a linen. Looking up at me, she spoke again. "My aunt is the healer's assistant. Your clansman is in good hands, my lord."

Duncan opened his eyes, glassy with pain and delirium. He looked over at her. "Beauty," he breathed.

She smiled softly down at him and wiped the linen across his face again. "Heal, warrior."

"Dragon," he muttered locking eyes with her. "I see... your dragon..."

Well that is a development, I thought.

"Aye, warrior, my dragon sees yours too. Get well and we will get to know one another," the female said.

He hummed a happy sound as his eyes closed and he fell unconscious.

"Thank you, lass," I said. "I know Duncan will be safe with you."

"He will," she confirmed. "Go to your king, my lord. He will have need of you. I saw the numbers. A dragon of your strength will surely be needed."

One last look at my friend, I hurried out of the room, down the hall, and through the Great Hall.

Breaking out of the keep, I searched for Finn. Seeing him across the bailey where he stood with our uncles looking up at the dragons who were attacking us, I shouted his name.

All three looked over at me and Raeghar and Teren took a stance stepping in front of the kings.

"He is rogue!" Teren shouted.

"Nay, wait!" Finn replied "I've seen this before. Cahal is still in control. He is safe."

I approached with as much caution as I could, but as soon as I was standing before them, I spoke to Finn.

"Duncan is badly injured. One of the boulders struck him. He is alive but both his legs are crushed. He will be of no use."

"Damnation," Finn muttered. "An attack on one of us was an attack on us all."

"What is happening, Finn?" I demanded.

"The Irish dragon king Tahra heard the men say?" Finn reminded me. I nodded. "It is our grandfather."

Chapter Ten

Finn

 could not express the relief I felt seeing Cahal awake and alive, but I had no time to welcome him. His eyes were slitted, and he looked rogue, but I knew it was the same as last time. He was in control and at the moment, we needed him. No other male, save Raeghar, was better at war strategy than he.

Clasping my brother's hand, I pulled him into a quick embrace. "Does my heart good to see you, brother. You are well?"

"For now, aye," he answered. "The dragon bane must still be in my system, but I have built a sort of immunity to it. My dragon may look to be in control but we both are. 'Tis an odd feeling."

"You must show me how that is done," Teren replied. "I could use the strategy."

"Aye, we all could," Raeghar stated.

"Do you have a plan?" I questioned seeing Drake's dragon form take another dragon from the sky before the boulder could be loosed.

"Aye," Rexian said. "I was just about to tell them. He wants me. This will not end until I give him what he wants."

"Absolutely not," Raeghar and Teren said together.

"It is the only way," Rexian said.

"Rexian, I forbid it," Raeghar spoke.

"You forget your place, brother," Rexian answered. "But I will let it go for now."

"Rae, now would be a good time to tell them what we discovered," Teren whispered, not so softly to my uncle.

The War Chief sent a side eye to his lieutenant.

"What have you discovered?" Rexian demanded.

The two males locked eyes before they spoke. Teren taking the lead. "My king, under advisement from your War Chief I have been making inquiries. There seemed to be too much of a coincidence that the attacks happened when we, or I should say, you, were at your weakest."

"And you were going to tell me when?"

"As soon as I had more information," Raeghar said.

"And what more information has come to light?"

Teren looked at Raeghar but waited for him to nod once. "Sire, there is someone in our midst who is not loyal to you."

"What do you mean?"

"I mean we have an informant," Teren said looking around.

"And who is it?"

"That we don't know yet," Raeghar replied.

"I wish you had come to me with this sooner."

"You had enough to worry about," Raeghar said. "Teren has it well in control."

"Your trust in me means more than I can say," Teren winked. Raeghar's eyes widened at his reaction but he chuckled and shook his head.

"But if you insist on this course of action, Rexian," Raeghar began. "You will need us all to watch your back."

"My intention is to bring him down for hand-to-hand combat in human form," Rexian explained.

"He'll never agree to that," Cahal said. "He's an old male. He'll never agree to human combat. He has no hope of winning."

"We each choose a champion, so it is not just us," Rexian offered.

"And your champion of choice?" Raeghar questioned.

"I would never ask you to kill our father."

"I am not loyal to him," Raeghar said.

"Then," Rexian replied. "You are my champion of course, brother."

"Good," Raeghar stated with a nod. "I agree then. But, you had better not need me."

"I will not." Rexian touched his brother's elbow in assurance then stepped forward, looking up at the sky, he shouted in his most vibrant voice. "Haeger, Father, Former King, I challenge you to human hand-to-hand combat, as is our way. Stop this now. Fight me for the throne. Choose a champion but stop this destruction."

All seemed to go silent as a grey dragon roared. Then slowly the dragon circled and landed. Two others landed beside him and once he shifted back to human, we saw our grandfather's form. Though his hair was white, his body and features looked like a male half his age.

"Oh Rexian, always the sacrifice," his smarmy voice said. "You always put yourself last and in so doing put the kingdom last. What do you think will happen when we fight to see who is strongest?"

"I expect one of us to die," Rexian stood, feet spread and arms crossed over his expansive chest.

"Indeed," Haeger stated sizing him up. "You said to choose a champion. Will we fight first, or will it be them?"

"Them," Raeghar stepped forward.

Rexian whirled around. "What are you doing?" He hissed.

"If you honestly thought I would be allowing you, my

king, to fight first you are very much mistaken," Raeghar said.

"I chose this, Raeghar, not you," Rexian replied.

"And I choose to not see my king and brother fight to his death."

"You think so little of me?"

"Nay, but I know him," his eyes flashed to their father. "He will cheat. He will do anything possible. At least with me fighting first he will not have the ability."

"Raeghar," Rexian breathed. "I cannot allow you to do this."

"Then don't, my king," Teren stepped forward. Raeghar whipped around. "Choose me."

"What do you think you are doing?" Raeghar sizzled.

"Same as you, I imagine," Teren replied. "Rexian, chose me."

"Nay," Raeghar spat. "I am the king's champion."

"And you mean more to me alive," Teren answered.

"I cannae have you do this," Raeghar replied. "He will find out."

"So be it," Teren said.

"Ter," Raeghar cautioned.

"If you think this will stop me, think again," he answered. "I've pinned you on your back many times, Raeghar and enjoyed doing it. Do you honestly think whatever champion the former king will choose is greater than you?"

"I forbid it," Raeghar said.

"Now who is being unreasonable?" Teren asked with a

fond smile.

"Enough," Haeger called. "I have chosen mine. Will you break up this little domestic scene and choose yours?"

My eyes snapped to my uncle. If this scene was as it sounded like, Raeghar and Teren... nay, I could nae believe it.

Rexian turned back to his father. "Teren. He is my champion," he said.

"Nay," Raeghar snapped.

Teren stepped forward next to his king.

"Well well, if you are so weak as to assume the role of docile king that I always knew you would, have your *champion* step forward to meet mine," Haeger said.

Teren took a step but Rexian shot out a hand to stop him. The back of his hand flush against Teren's chest. Raeghar growled.

"If you think you can best me, *father*," he spat. "Let us ignore our champions and fight each other."

"Gladly," Haeger replied.

Teren looked back at Raeghar whose body looked ready to pounce.

All fell silent as Rexian and Haeger circled each other.

"Stand back everyone," Rexian ordered. "By order of your king. Whatever the outcome you will accept it."

"Oh, they will have no choice," Haeger stated and lunged toward his son.

Rexian dodged the sloppy attempt. The dragons and dragonmen in human form created a circle around the two males.

"Stupid fool." Raeghar jerked forward attempting to stop them but Teren held him back. The more I watched them, the more I realized their relationship. They knew each other very well, better than any platonic relationship. They were clearly lovers or something equally as intimate. Still, the idea was foreign to me, but I had no time to think on it. My grandfather rushed toward my uncle and soon, they were scuffling on the ground.

My uncle got a few good hits, but my grandfather was stronger than I had assumed, and he soon had my uncle pinned beneath him and was landing strong blows.

"You're weak," he seethed. "You're making a mockery of my throne."

Rexian got the upper hand by twisting in his father's grip and using his weight to flip him over.

"You're an old man and a fool," Rexian spewed. "You think you're a god. We serve as king because we are our clan's choice. We serve at their pleasure not the other way around. You cannot keep males and females in servitude and not expect them to rise up against you."

My grandfather landed a blow to my uncle's temple, stunning him for a moment.

"And what?" my grandfather chastised. "You want to be everyone's friend? You are king? Act like it!"

"I am more king than you, old man," Rexian spewed gaining the upper hand again by flipping them both over.

"I thought killing your true mate would kill you. But apparently you didn't love her as much as everyone thought you did."

Rexian froze for a split second but it was a split second

too long. Grandfather used it to his advantage and hit my uncle again on the temple. They both reared back and my uncle fell on his rear. Haeger stood and towered over him.

"That's right, lad." The venom in his words hit my heart. "She was killed by someone loyal to me. Slowly. Over time. And when the time came for her bastard to be born, well, the poison did its work."

A hush blew through the bailey as my grandfather's words sunk in. Then, my uncle bellowed louder than I had ever heard before and shifted in a single moment. Beating his wings, he lifted off the ground and rose high in the sky. Before my grandfather had a chance to shift, Rexian blew out his fire, reducing his father to ash.

The silence echoed across the bailey as Rexian landed and slowly shifted back. The males loyal to my grandfather watched with bitter anticipation.

"This male killed my true mate. My queen. Your queen. Those of you who believe my punishment was ill advised, may leave now without retribution. You have my word; no harm will come to you. But if you would pledge your loyalty to me, you will be welcome," Rexian's voice was tight with pain but strong with fervor.

One by one the males loyal to my grandfather formed a line. Rexian's eyes held on one dragon in particular.

"Brother," he called. "Florian, you are welcome back, if you so desire."

The dragon snorted and took to the sky. Rexian shook his head and sighed.

Raeghar and Teren walked over to him. "You idiot," Raeghar breathed as he embraced his brother.

"You have so little faith in me, brother?" Rexian questioned.

"Nay, but I would have gladly done it."

"And lived your life with the memory of killing your own father? Nay, it was mine to avenge. Niamh can rest peacefully now."

"I cannot believe it, majesty," Teren replied. "I watched our queen day and night, and no one would be able to poison her. Who could it be?"

"Whoever it is," Rexian sighed. "We will discover them. For now, I have clansmen to welcome."

"Be careful, your majesty," Teren said. "We have yet to find the dragon responsible."

"My father killed my mate, Teren," he replied. "Do you honestly think I care?"

"Still, sire, go gently," he said.

"I thank you for your caution," he answered. "Now, if you'll excuse me."

Rexian walked over to the steps of the keep. Teren walked behind him. They stood, welcoming those who were pledging their loyalty. Some took to the air and flew away from the castle, but others were lining up to speak with Rexian. Raeghar and I exchanged a look.

"He's an endearing fool," Raeghar said with a smile. "But still a fool."

"So you've said," I answered. Then after a beat, I spoke again. "Uncle, are you... happy with Teren?"

He crossed his arms but did not look at me, instead his

eyes were on Rexian and Teren.

"I suppose you think I'm... unnatural," he said.

"Honestly, I donnae care one way or the other, so long as he makes you happy."

He paused and smiled. "Aye, *he* does."

"Then, I'm happy for you."

"Good," he stated.

"It is odd, I'll not deny, but I donnae care one way or the other," I said.

"Again, good," he replied, his eyes moving for a moment from his lieutenant and brother to mine.

The brief moment he locked eyes with me was all it took. We both heard the screams as one of the warriors in Raeghar's army broke ranks and rushed toward Rexian. The king turned, clearly shocked to see one of his own but he did nothing to stop it.

"Sire!" Teren shouted as he stepped in front of him.

Blocking the one knife, he did not see the other wee dagger in the male's hands. The warrior struck out and all seemed to stop at Teren's gasp. Raeghar whipped around screaming "Nay!" as soon as he saw his lover struck.

Teren's gaze fell on him as he held the wrist of the warrior who stabbed him.

"I'm sorry," Teren mouthed as he looked at Raeghar.

"Nay!" Raeghar screamed again and raced toward Teren as other dragons surrounded the one who stabbed him and overpowered him.

Raeghar slid on his knees and held Teren. "Nay, Ter, stay

with me."

The horrid gurgling sound Teren made gave me chills as I watched my uncle rock back and forth with his warrior's body.

"My lord!" a female pushed through the gathered dragons. "My lord, let me help her."

"Her?" Cahal and I questioned at the same time.

"Please, save her," Raeghar begged the female as she reached them.

"I will. The wound is deep but it is not so deep as to be life threatening," the female said. "May I see?"

Raeghar removed his hand over Teren's abdomen and the female checked the wound. Teren reared up in pain.

"Stay with me, Ter," Raeghar begged. "Please."

"Shh shh," Teren reached up and cupped Raeghar's face. "It takes more than a knife wound to get rid of me. The king?"

"Safe," Raeghar pronounced.

"The wound is already healing, sire," the old healer said. "She will be fine."

Raeghar let out a loud sigh of relief and buried his head in Teren's hair. "Thank the gods."

"See? Can't get rid of me that easily, true mate," Teren stated. "After everything I've done to be near to you? This is nothing."

"I never requested it," Raeghar replied. "I love you the way you are."

"I know," Teren said. "And I am glad for it."

"Brother," Rexian cautiously approached. Raeghar's

eyes snapped to the king as if seeing everyone staring for the first time.

"Rexian," his hoarse voice said.

"Go to him," Teren replied. "I'll be fine."

Reverently, Raeghar set Teren down and in the care of the healer. He stood and faced his brother, his head bowed.

"Walk with me," Rexian ordered. Raeghar agreed and looked back at Teren once more. "Finn, you are in control. Cahal come with us."

Cahal glanced at me and I noticed his eyes were back to human. He looked at me for approval and once I nodded, knowing he would tell me everything later, Cahal walked with our uncles and I turned back to the clan.

Cahal

I walked with my uncles into the keep, through the Great Hall, and up to the King's Solar. It took a long moment for either of my uncles to speak. Rexian poured large glasses of whiskey for us and motioned for us to sit. Raeghar said nothing, only waited for Rexian.

"What is her real name?" Rexian finally asked.

"Terena," Raeghar replied.

"And you didn't think to tell me about this at all? You are War Chief there is a reason why that position is unmateable. It can be used against you."

"I didn't know," Raeghar admitted. "Ter was introduced as the long-lost son of her parents and as I was fostering with another clan as a lad I thought it was true. I truly didn't know. I didn't understand my... infatuation with him. Her." He shook his head.

"Tell me everything."

Raeghar let out a long-suffering sigh and downed half of his whiskey. "I met Teren five years ago. She was dressed as a male, short hair, trousers. She bound her bosom, so she was not noticed. Even her scent was not quite male not quite female masked with lemon water. She was a good warrior. The best warrior I had ever met. She bested me on the battle ground twice. I didn't understand my... physical reaction to her when she pinned me. It was embarrassing. I thought I was... I took to following her. She rose through the ranks quickly as you ken. But I always thought it odd how she would never shift in front of others. She claimed it was because she was raised by a human parent and therefore nakedness was taboo. But one time I followed her to see what happened and found her bathing in a spring. Her... female attributes on full display. I confronted her about it and that was when I realized."

"Realized what?" I asked after he stayed silent for a while.

"I could see her dragon behind her eyes." Raeghar looked down.

"She's your true mate?" Rexian questioned.

"She is."

"Why didn't you tell me?"

"How would it be? Your War Chief not only falling for his lieutenant but having a female in the group of warriors? They are all capable but war is no place for them. To have been taken in by her... made a mockery of? Nay, Rexian, I could not tell you."

"And all those secret meetings, little looks between you

both? She is your lover. Do not deny it."

"We... I will not have you disparage the lass." Raeghar stood.

"I am not the one who lied about this."

"You are right," Raeghar replied. "I did lie. For five years I lied to you. All the times we were in conference together, we were... aye, we were lovers. We *are* lovers. And I'll not ask for forgiveness because I do not believe there is any reason. She is my true mate and I'll be damned if I cannot be with her. I kept her secret because I have never met a warrior like her. I kept her secret because she deserves her title as my lieutenant."

"Are you sure she deserves it? Or is she leading you around by your bollocks, brother?"

Raeghar reared back and his fist collided with Rexian's jaw. I stood ready to hold my uncle back but he seemed to realize what he had done and stepped back, his head lowered in supplication.

"I see your levelheadedness has taken leave of you," Rexian stated rubbing his jaw. "I could have you arrested for that."

Raeghar said nothing, only nodded.

"You would be willing to throw all of this away for her? Your life, your career, your family."

"She is my family too." Raeghar looked up at him, his eyes dark with pain. "I love her more than words can express. But she was willing to sacrifice herself for you. Her loyalty is clear."

"And yours is not?"

"You know you have my loyalty. Always. But there are

times when I wonder, brother. You are so blinded by your grief. Do you want us all to be alone?"

Rexian stared at him. "You chose to fight for the title of War Chief knowing it is unmateable. You were the one who willfully lied to me. Tell me true, brother. What do you think my reaction would have been if you had told me that first instant you knew? That instant you saw her dragon? What would I have done?"

Raeghar searched his brother's face. "I believe you would have helped me."

"And yet, you chose to lie?"

"For her. She deserves every accolade. Everything. She is an incredible warrior."

"A fact she has proven time and time again," Rexian said. "So do you truly think I would have sent her away? Stripped her of that title simply because she was a woman? I am not our father, Raeghar. I would not have cared one way or the other. But for you to willfully lie to me... that is where I draw the line."

Raeghar looked down. "I am sorry." He took a deep breath. "You have my resignation, my king. I will no longer be your War Chief, if you so desire it. But I beg you, let my punishment be an end of it. Leave Terena out of this. She has done nothing in all of this. She loves you and our queen. She would sneak from my bed to her room to check on her and stand watch outside her door to protect her when you were not there. She was gutted when Niamh died. We both were. How could we lord something like the true mate bond over you when you had just suffered the loss of your own? Please, I beg you. Let Terena be free of this folly. She saved you just now."

Rexian stared at him for a long time, clearly searching

for something in his face.

"Do you love her?" He finally asked.

"More than life."

Rexian paused, the thin lines appearing around his lips were the only outward form of emotion I could see on his face.

"Then, that is punishment enough," Rexian said. Raeghar looked up at his brother. "I cannot condone your mating. You are War Chief. It is not done. But if you can swear to me your relationship will not alter your judgement in anyway, then you have my blessing to maintain it. But it will be unsanctioned by the council and king."

Raeghar let out a breath. "You will allow it?"

"I will. I have seen a difference in you whenever she is around. Niamh..." his voice choked around his late mate's name. "Niamh," he continued. "Always knew there was something more about her. She must have known. I have had the love of my life, I can never prevent someone from experiencing it themselves. Though again, I cannot give my War Chief in marriage, I do bless your union but caution you. Do not let anything else come of this that might be able to be used against you. There is a reason a War Chief has no mate nor whelps."

Raeghar nodded. "It is not a problem. She is... unable to carry them. An accident as a young female prevents her from conceiving."

"Good," Rexian said. "Now, I do believe you owe me a strike."

Raeghar agreed. "Aye, my king, I am sorry I hit you."

"I do believe an extra shift on the battlements every night for a month should remedy it."

"That's it?" Raeghar questioned.

"Aye," Rexian replied, a small smile lifting the corner of his mouth. "You are my brother. But you are more than that. Without you and Elyan, I would not be here. That in itself warrants all the forgiveness in the world. Now, come, introduce me to your true mate properly and let us be done with this."

Raeghar's breathing increased and I swore I saw a shimmer of a tear track on his cheek as he grabbed his brother's shoulder and pulled him into an embrace.

"Thank you," he mumbled.

"Enough, you're sappy enough without handing me your bollocks on a silver platter," Rexian teased pulling back.

"Uncles," I piped up. "Forgive me, but what are we going to do with the humans and other dragons? We surely cannae allow them to go about without punishment."

"I intend to banish Korlon from my lands."

"Aye, but what about those who are loyal to him? There needs to be something else to make sure no further action is taken," I offered.

"What do you have in mind, lad?"

"Well," I began. "The treaty needs to be such that no amount of time or weapons can break it."

"And why do I feel you have a treaty in mind?" Raeghar asked.

"Because I might have an answer to it, Uncle." I grinned. "There just might be a precedent I am familiar with on Skye."

"I am all ears, son."

Chapter Eleven

Finn

They were gone much longer than I expected. And I found myself answering questions from some of the females who had left the confines of the queen's solar when they realized the battle was over. They wanted to know where certain males were and though I did nae ken who they meant, I strove to assist them however I could. I was grateful beyond belief to see Teren... or whatever his... *Her* name was, stand on her own and color return to her cheeks. The more I observed her, the more I saw the feminine side of her. Her cheeks, chin, and jaw were smooth with no amount of hair, unlike others; even my Uncle Raeghar had a full face of closely trimmed dark spiky hair. I scrubbed my jaw without thought and felt the prickly nature that showed after a few days of not shaving. Teren's body, though well shaped for a warrior, was curvier and less like the square of a male's torso. Looking at her neck, there was no pronounced bump indicative of males. It was clear she was a female. What was unclear was why she pretended and why no one had noticed before.

"My lord," I heard a familiar female voice say. Turning to her, I bowed slightly when I saw my mate's mother walk up to me. "Have you seen Elyan?"

"I am here, love," my uncle called from beside one of the boulders that had landed in the bailey. He was attempting to remove the heavy stone to assess the damage made to the smithy.

Connifarrah breathed a sigh of relief and hurried to him. They embraced and Elyan kissed his mate. Taking a moment, I watched them. Questions of how I was going to tell Brigid, what I would even say, entered my mind. It was not going to be easy, and I worried for her health and that of my whelp. But Cahal's response came back to me. Brigid is strong. She deserved to know what happened to her mother. And no matter what happened, I would be there for her. Always.

As the crowd grew, I assisted my cousin Cinaeth clear some of the destruction and helped two of the more injured warriors seeking a healer. Our numbers sacrificed one and when he was found, we all mourned. A young life, but one I did not know. His mother wailed for him as he was pulled out of the lough, his throat torn out. I barely contained the bile that threatened in my throat. He looked so like Bearcbhan. The memory of carrying my brother's body to my father was still fresh in my mind.

I felt a presence next to me and looked over to see Cahal had arrived. We stared at the body before bowing our heads in respect for the fallen life. Cahal's knuckles brushed mine and for a moment his comfort was all I needed. We still had each other. Rexian walked over to us as Raeghar went to the body. The War Chief pulled out a medallion from his pocket and placed it over the warrior's chest.

"A token from the War Chief for his sacrifice. Raeghar has made it a tradition," Rexian explained. "Damn shame. He was to be mated this next year. A good lad."

"We are sorry for your loss, Uncle," Cahal said.

"Raeghar will take it harder than I do. He always does."

We both watched as Teren walked over to our uncle and slipped her hand in his. Raeghar's usually tall and proud personage was slumped as if he held the weight of the battle on his shoulders. In a way, he did.

The lad was taken back to his family's cottage and laid out for burial. Rexian called for all those who were able, to come inside to the Great Hall for food and ale to keep their strength up. The meal was somber as all dragons present, ate in silence, the atmosphere heavy.

"Uncle Raeghar isn't joining us?" I asked.

"No, he doesn't when there's a death. It's, well, I never understood but now I do, he and Teren... I'm sorry, Terena, discuss arrangements. I suppose it is her way of helping him through," Rexian revealed.

"Will you tell me the story? I was not privy to it." I took

a drink of ale as Cahal and Rexian launched into the narrative. Their story surprised me, but I was happy to learn of Uncle Raeghar's happiness. Though my uncle held to the old way of thinking that a War Chief could not mate nor have whelps because of the commitment and the threat of abduction and coercion, I was pleased my father had changed his theory and was allowing Kai to marry Tahra. The thought of getting home soon for their mating ceremony, itched in the back of my mind. We had been here long enough. It was time to go home.

Raeghar and Teren... Terena appeared at the stair and caught Rexian's eyes. They nodded once and Rexian leaned back.

"I know you lads are wanting to head home, but there is one more thing I need from you," Rexian said.

"Anything, Uncle," I replied.

"I need a mediator," he looked pointedly at Cahal who agreed.

"We will meet you, Uncle," Cahal said. "Let me tell Finn what we discussed. He knows the treaty better than anyone."

"Good," Rexian stood. "I will meet you in my solar in ten minutes."

Once our uncle left the area followed by Raeghar, Terena, Elyan, and Cinaeth, I leaned closer to my brother.

"What treaty?"

"Negotiations between Korlon's people and the dragons to end this bitter feud."

"And why did you say I would know more about this?" I asked.

"Because we are considering the same sort of treaty we

had with the Lewis."

I leaned back. "A marriage treaty."

"Indeed."

Nodding slowly, "it might work," I said.

"That is why I need you. You studied the treaty before you went to claim Brigid. You know it better than anyone here."

"That is true," I acquiesced. "But do you honestly think Korlon would be amenable to such a notion?"

"Uncle Rexian has been approached by one of Korlon's males. Apparently, he and many are not loyal to Korlon but to his late father," Cahal explained. "They are only too willing to see justice done as they believe Korlon killed his father for the lairdship."

"Would not surprise me," I admitted. "That male is evil."

"So we have arranged a meeting between those who will take over since Korlon has been sentenced to death."

"Death?" I questioned.

"Aye, Uncle will decree it after the treaty is signed."

"Good," I growled. The male tried to take my sister; I would shed no tear at his execution nor would I try to stop it. "Do you think they will accept such a treaty?"

"I do," Cahal answered. "But we will see. Uncle wants you to lead the discussion."

"Easily," I agreed. We stood and headed up the stairs to the king's solar.

Two dragons and three human warriors stood outside the door. The dragons bowed to Finn and opened the door for him. We entered seeing our uncles standing, speaking to three human males, one of whom looked much older but still fighting fit.

"Ah, my lords, these are my nephews, King Aodhfionn of the Isle of Skye and Lord Cahal his most trusted advisor," Rexian introduced. "Nephews, you know your Uncle Talisian of course, this is Kenmare the War Chief of the clan and his son Tomas. We were just discussing the inevitable fate of their former lord. Korlon's execution will be held tomorrow when the sun is at its highest. But before then, we want to announce a treaty that has been struck between our two clans."

"My brother informed me of this, Uncle," I replied. "I would be happy to speak of the treaty we have found so useful on Skye."

I took the seat Rexian offered and began speaking of the treaty we had with the Lewis clan and how every twenty years a human from the village was given in marriage to one of our dragonmen. I made sure to stress the importance of the female understanding what was to happen and how it was required she chose it freely and unreservedly.

"And your marriages?" Kenmare asked. "They are happy and successful?"

"They are, I am happy to say. My own mate... wife, is one such lass. We still have several females who have been with us for varying times, the eldest of which is still mated to her male and has been with our clan for sixty years."

"What of the age difference?" Tomas asked. "Is it true you dragons live longer than most humans?"

"We can," I replied. "But when a human female mates with one of our males and bares their whelp... child, the hormones of the child seep into the mother we believe. The females live extended lives healthy and happy. When a dragon males mates, it is for life and when our females pass, a part of us pass too if not actually die with her." A subtle glance over to my uncle showed his face pale and hands trembling. He closed his eyes for a moment before Elyan stepped beside him and placed a comforting hand on his back.

"And how are the women treated?" Kenmare asked.

I grinned. "It is clear, if you don't mind me saying so, my lord that you have not been around dragon males when their mates are near."

"I have not," he chuckled. "But from the look in your eye I would imagine it is quite the sight."

"Our females are treasured. They want for nothing and are given every right males have. They can deny their mates if they desire and can request for a mating to end. They are loved beyond measure and we like to show that to them."

"What of childbearing?" Tomas asked. "It is laborious for our own women when their time comes, is it harder or more difficult for your wives?"

Rexian coughed, clearly covering a whimper.

"It is the same," I admitted. "There are risks and complications for all, but I will say it is rare."

Rexian turned to the sideboard and poured himself a large glass of whiskey.

"I am sorry, your majesty, to put you through this. I heard of the recent loss of your wife," Kenmare offered.

Rexian accepted his apology with a wave of his hand but did not turn. All the dragons in the room could smell the pain he was feeling.

"If we were to accept this treaty," Tomas went on. "Who among you would marry the human woman?"

"That is something we would need to discuss as I am sure you would need to speak with the female who will accept," I said.

"I have someone in mind," Tomas answered. "But I would need your assurance of who would be the one. I want her with someone of power. She's a young woman of title."

"We will be able to negotiate," Rexian finally turned. "But I can assure you it will not be me, nor will it be any of my brothers."

"You are unmated," Tomas stated.

"Tomas," his father chastised. "Show respect. He lost his mate."

"But he is still unmated," Tomas said to his father. "And I will have no one unworthy with Anne."

Cinaeth jolted. "Anne?"

"Aye, my sister," Tomas replied. "She was to marry Korlon but since he will not be around much longer, not that I will shed a tear for him, I want to be assured of her position."

"And I would have your word it would be her?" Cinaeth questioned.

"Of course," Tomas answered.

"Then, father," Cinaeth stepped forward addressing Rexian. "I volunteer."

"You?" Rexian's brows drew together. "Cinaeth you're nineteen."

"And Anne is eighteen. I will have no other with her,"

Cinaeth stated. Everyone in the room went silent. Cinaeth appeared to grow into a grown male before our eyes. His strength was unmated.

"Who is she to you?" Rexian asked softly. "For certs, you've never mentioned her."

"There was no reason to," Cinaeth explained. "She was betrothed to another."

"But?" his father asked.

"But," Cinaeth sighed. "She is my true mate." The dragons paused.

"You know my sister? How?" Tomas asked.

"I met her by accident, my lord," Cinaeth replied turning to him. "She was too far on our side of the wall and I was on patrol. I dropped and shifted behind a tree to ask if she was in need of anything. I assure you, once I was properly attired in my trews and shirt did I step out, she saw nothing. I understand that is not the way for humans. She told me she was daydreaming and did not realize where she was."

"She daydreams much," Kenmare laughed.

"I escorted her home. It was merely an hour, but I was enchanted. We met many times after that. I apologize I did not tell you, Father, but I assure you both, she is my true mate."

"She wouldn't stop speaking of dragons," Tomas chuckled. "I though she was fascinated by them but now I realize why. I did not know it was because she met one."

"What does the term *true mate* mean?" Kenmare asked.

"It is a term used to describe the one the gods have ordained for us. We know who our true mate is, and therefore our best opportunity for happiness, when they see our dragon behind our eyes and if she is a dragon, we can see hers," Raeghar replied.

"And my daughter can see your dragon?" Kenmare questioned.

"She can," Cinaeth confirmed. "She mentioned it on our third meeting. I knew then she was my true mate."

"And you are certain you want to do this, son?" Rexian asked.

"Very certain, Father," he replied.

Rexian then turned to Kenmare and Tomas. "What say you?"

"How can I deny my daughter the love of a true mate?" Kenmore asked. "Aye, I agree. Son?"

Tomas locked eyes with Rexian.

"Her position is assured. She will be queen one day," Rexian said.

"Aye, my sister Anne and your son Cinaeth will be a suitable match," Tomas replied.

"Draw up the treaty, we will sign. Our people will rejoice, and Tomas will go and bring Anne and my wife here. We shall have a wedding soon," Kenmare decreed.

"Nephew," Rexian began looking at me. "Will you draw up the treaty?"

"I will need parchment, a quill and ink."

"Done." Rexian then offered his arm in a warrior's shake to Kenmare and his son. "And we will rejoice with you. My son is an excellent male."

"I have no doubt of it," Kenmore stated. "But if I may,

Majesty, may I have a moment alone with my daughter's future husband?"

Rexian grinned devilishly and we all knew full well the conversation. As we hurried out of the room, I glanced back to see my cousin swallow audibly and stare at his future father-by-mating and I chuckled. Every male feared getting and giving the future father talk.

Chapter Twelve

Cahal

Once the ink was dry on the treaty, Rexian made the announcement of Korlon's execution and Tomas left to get his mother and sister. Korlon went to his death sniveling, begging for mercy but the execution was swift which was more than he deserved. Considering he was going to force my sister and steal her innocents all because he thought it would mean he commanded us across the water, I cared not for his feeble cries. If that made me the monster I always fought, so be it.

Anne and Cinaeth's mating ceremony took place the next day and Finn and I stayed with our uncles another night before deciding it was time to head home. As we broke our fast the day after the wedding, I was nae surprised when I did not see my cousin join us.

"Shirking his duty again," Raeghar chuckled looking at the empty seat on the dais.

"Come now, brother," Rexian teased. "You should know what it's like not wanting to leave a lass nor the warmth of your bed."

Terena laughed at his blush. "Truth, sire," she said, still dressed in her trousers but looking a little less like a male than when we first met her. "'Tis I who have to kick his sorry arse out of bed."

"I don't doubt it," Rexian laughed.

"Enough now," Raeghar grumbled. "It is unseemly for a female to speak so vulgarly."

"Oh indeed?" Terena questioned. "And here I was hoping revealing who I was would not change you, Rae. It appears, I was wrong. You thought nothing when I heralded my *conquests* amongst the males, however fake they might have been."

"Fake?" I questioned.

"I couldn't rightly describe bedding a lass from experience, now could I?" she grinned. "Not as a male. I noticed Raeghar blush a few times when I described what he had done to me the night before."

"Ter," Raeghar warned again, face as red as a cherry.

"He's such a prude," she teased. "He said nothing on my experiences then."

"Because I knew them to be fake. But now—"

"You know they're not, as they involve you and our bed?"

"Our bed?" he asked.

She shrugged. "'Twould do little to lie about where I've been the last few nights."

"Recovering."

"Oh, is that the story we are telling? So sorry, I didn't know. Shall I also not mention how you're forcing me to *recover* naked and in your arms?" She asked.

Raeghar choked on his morning watered down ale and sputtered as it blew across the table. Terena gently thumped his back helping him.

"There now, poor dear."

"My brother has no concept what he has created." Rexian laughed.

"No indeed, sire," she replied.

"And on that happy topic," Finn said standing. "I am afraid we must leave you, Uncle."

I stood beside my brother as our uncles and the others at the king's table pushed back from their seats.

"I understand Elyan and Connifarrah join you," Rexian broached the subject I knew my brother was still wary of.

"Indeed. I agreed to let them come with us since they threatened to make the journey on their own. I only pray Brigid is well enough to hear the news her mother is still alive," Finn said.

"All will be well," Rexian promised. "We will miss you." He embraced us both.

"And we will miss you, Uncle," Finn replied. "Do keep us updated on when you become a grandfather." Finn winked causing our uncle to pale and then laugh.

"Send me word when your mate whelps," he told Finn. "My good wishes go with you. Please say hello to everyone for us."

"We will," Finn promised and turned to Raeghar and Terena.

Our uncle's mate stood and embraced Finn. "It was so wonderful to meet you both," she said. "And thank you for supporting us."

"The honor was mine, my lady," Finn bowed slightly. "You must come to Skye soon so our mother can meet you."

"Our intentions are after your mate whelps," Raeghar said. "'Twould be good to see everyone again."

"You are always welcome," Finn stated looking at everyone on the dais.

After smiling and thanking Finn, Rexian looked over at me with a soft look. "'Twas good to see you, lad."

"And you, Uncle," I said. "Please be sure to write. I missed receiving your letters."

"I will. And you, let me know how things progress with your mate."

"Very hopefully, things will progress well," I said.

Raeghar placed a hand on my shoulder. "I know we will

be happy to hear it. Remember what I said on our walk, Cahal. Work with her not against what Bearcbhan was to her."

"Sound advice, my love," Terena agreed. "And from what I know of the situation, Cahal, which admittedly is not much, she loves you. She always has and always will."

"I was reminded of that just the other day," I admitted remembering my brief conversation with Bearcbhan. "Thank you, all. I will keep your council in mind as I see my mate again."

"I want to check in with Duncan before we leave," Finn said. "He's never been on an adventure by himself and I am certain he will find this an... eye opening experience."

We grinned. Duncan, the quiet, shy male had found his true mate and she was fiery.

Checking on our healer, I was happy to see he looked healthy, though he was unable to move his legs as the shattered bones knit back together. His mate sat beside him, wiping his brow when sweat broke out as he tried to sit up to greet his king.

"Donnae get up," Finn said. "We merely wanted to check on you, Duncan. 'Tis glad I am you look better than you did just yesterday."

"The help of a wonderful female, sire," he replied looking over at her. "Have you met Rivany?"

"I have. You were unconscious for most of the time, Duncan," Finn said. "You will take good care of my healer, lass?"

"I will, your majesty," she swore. "He means much to me already."

"I can see that." Finn placed his hand on Duncan's

shoulder. "Get well soon, lad."

"I will. Thank you, sire," he said. "Safe journey home."

And with that, we met our kin in the bailey, said goodbye once more, shifted, and flew to meet our males who had gathered the camp across the water. I knew Finn was still leery of having Elyan and Connifarrah join us, but as his golden dragon followed just behind us, carrying a basket with Connifarrah inside, Finn decidedly did not look back at our uncle.

We were home in a day and were greeted to fanfare as we landed in the bailey. Mother, Father, Tahra, Sybine, Brigid, Kai, and many of our warriors' mates or families stood near us. Finn tipped his head back and blew out his white fire on a roar. The dragons followed. A symbol to show, we were home.

Chapter Thirteen

Finn

I worried greatly for my mate. I saw her rush out of the keep to greet me, the broad beaming smile she graced my way, made my chest ache. I loved her so very much and I could never imagine a life without her. My uncle's pain of losing his true mate flashed before my eyes as I looked down and took in how heavily swollen her stomach was. I tilted my head to the side confused. I was only gone not even a week and she looked larger than usual. That scared me even more. If the whelp was too large for her...

"Welcome home, my king, my husband," she stepped forward and her voice sounded strong and beautiful on the wind.

I bowed my head to her and began to shift. When it was safe, she brought me a plaid and I wrapped it around my hips.

"Our males are all accounted for save one," I spoke the traditional roll call. "Duncan is alive, but he was injured. He is set to make a full recovery and happy news," I turned to his parents who stood to my left. "He has found his true mate and she is a wonderful female for him."

His parents beamed happily knowing he was well and for the happy news.

"I am pleased to have you home," Brigid said and kissed me for the clan to see. It was a silly tradition but a tradition, nonetheless. It was customary for the queen to greet her husband and king in just the way she did and for the king to give the tally of either deaths or losses, then she was to welcome him home. I had seen my parents for many years engage in the tradition and was prouder than ever to know my mate had learned the protocols in my absence.

"I am beyond pleased to be home, my love," I whispered to her as I embraced her. "You are well?"

"I feel perfectly fit, my love. Tired of course, but our healer and I agree it is typical."

"I see you have grown while I've been away."

"Your son takes up much room, but it is a joy."

I rubbed her nose with mine in a soft gesture. "Males!" I shouted and turned, raising one arm in a fist over my head. "We are home!"

The dragon roar around me was deafening but it also ignited my blood in pride of my heritage. After my announcement, the males were able to shift and greet their families. The sounds that lit up around us were filled with joy. I took Brigid in my arms again and watched as my brother greeted Sybine. To my everlasting happiness, Sybine jumped into his arms and kissed him. Cahal caught her though surprised, and I saw the instant he relaxed and kissed his mate in return.

Greeting my parents, sister, and War Chief, I had little time to do anything else. I had promised Elyan and Connifarrah, who waited in the clearing just beyond our tree line that I would bring Brigid as soon as I could.

"Anything to report, Chief?" I asked Kai.

"Nothing, sire, all was right with our world," Kai announced.

"Good," I said. "I have to show Brigid something in the clearing. A gift I brought for her. Would you be willing to direct the servants to lay food? We will not be long."

"Of course," my mother stepped forward. "Your mate has made sure everything is prepared. We will begin pouring ale and wine if that is well with you, my queen."

Brigid looked up at my mother who still stood on the top stair next to my father and sister. "I promise, Erina I will never get used to you calling me that. Please do as you see fit. You know far better than I."

"Nonsense, my dear," she smiled sweetly at her. "You are

our queen now and I am so very happy for it. But for now, enjoy your gift and we will meet you back here in a short while."

"Thank you, Mama," I said and took Brigid's hand.

"Will you need a warrior or two, my king?" Kai asked.

"Not this time, Kai," I replied and walked with my mate out the bailey and into the woods surrounding us, praying with every step I was doing the right thing.

"What is the mystery, Finn?" Brigid asked. "I would much rather have shown you to our bedchamber. I had a bath drawn for you."

"You think of me always, my love," I said. "I promise I will make it up to you but I believe this is something you must see."

"See? Did you bring me a dragon horde or something?" She teased.

"Or something," I said then stopped. "Brig," my pet name for her made her smile. "You know I would do nothing to hurt you or our whelp. You know that, right?"

Her brow furrowed. "Of course. Dear me, what is going on?"

"I need you to prepare yourself. It will be a shock and I worry overmuch for the whelp and your safety."

"Finn, you're scaring me."

"Then I have already failed as that is the last thing I want to do."

She cupped my jaw and forced me to look into her eyes. After a moment, she spoke again. "Your dragon is pacing, Aodhfionn. What could possibly worry you so? I am fine. Our whelp is fine. Firmly tucked in his mother's body. All will be well."

"I pray you are right."

She reached up and kissed me softly. "Bring me to your surprise. And I promise you, my love, I will not let it hurt our child."

Taking a deep breath, I nodded and we walked on a little further. Once we reached the clearing, I saw my uncle and Connifarrah. Elyan was watching for us, having heard us as we approached. Fortunately in his human form with a tunic and trews covering him, he stood from a fallen tree when we broke through the tree line.

"Farrah," he called to his mate who was pacing, many scents wafted off her; fear, pain, regret, hope, worry it was dizzying.

Connifarrah whirled around and shrieked covering her mouth with her hand as her eyes fell on Brigid and instantly filled with tears.

"Brigid?" she breathed.

Brigid leaned into me for a brief moment. I watched her intently making sure I was there if she needed me and making sure none of it was too much for her. She was observing the female before her, her head tilted slightly to one side, closer to me. Her grip on my hand increased. I was sure if I were human the squeeze would be almost painful.

"I..." Connifarrah began. "I know you probably donnae ken me, lass."

"I do but I donnae," Brigid said. "It is strange. I feel I should know you." She looked up at me.

"Brigid, this is my Uncle Elyan from Ireland. He is my Uncle the king's most trusted advisor. And this is his mate, Connifarrah," I explained.

"But that wasn't my name given to me at birth," Farrah said. "It was the name given to me when I was injured and did nae ken who I was. Elyan," she looked back at him and he stood, wrapping and arm around her waist. "He found me and took me to his clan. He saved my life and I owe him much."

"You owe me nothing, Farrah," he whispered and kissed her hair.

"What was your name given at birth?" Brigid asked. Her voice wavering for a moment.

Connifarrah took a breath and held her mate's hand, much like Brigid held mine. "My name was Mirren Lewis and I was married to Brochan Lewis the War Chief of the Lewis Clan. I am your mother."

Brigid stared at her for a long moment then leaned into me as her eyes rolled back and she fainted.

I shouted her name as I caught her to me. Elyan rushed forward to assist and slowly we got her to the ground. I held her tightly to me speaking her name again and again. Connifarrah hurried over after a short moment. She was using a mortar and crushing herbs. Strong scent of mint, pine, and lavender hit my nose.

"Have her smell this, my lord," she offered.

It was only in that moment I remembered she was a healer like Brigid. I smelled it first to make sure all was well, but it made my head spin.

"It's strong herbs to help her wake," Connifarrah said.

I gently waved the cup under my mate's nose and Brigid coughed but opened her eyes.

"Finn!" she cried as soon as she could speak and then looked over at Connifarrah. "Finn," she breathed softly clutching my arms. "Mother?"

"Aye, my dearest one," Connifarrah said. "You're all right, love. Just a little shock. You're fine."

"How?" she whispered.

"It is a long story, dearling," Connifarrah moved Brigid's hair out of her face. "But I am true and I am here."

"Tell me," she slowly sat up in my arms, leaning her back to my chest. "Tell me something only you would know."

"What would you like me to say? What would convince you?"

Brigid thought a long moment. "Tell me what it was about me you claimed I would grow to resent one day."

Connifarrah chuckled sadly. "Your fiery temper, love. So like your da'. But I also told you that one day that fire will save you. You are your father's daughter but you are also a Dragon Queen. I am so proud of you, my love."

"Mama?" she questioned again, this time with tears in her eyes. "Oh mama!"

"My dearest," Connifarrah accepted her in her arms as Brigid shot out of mine and into her mother's.

Both women wept for a long time. Elyan and I beside them both offering what silent reassurances we could.

"But how?" Brigid finally questioned pulling back. "How is this possible? I was told you were burned at the stake."

"I was told you drown in the loch," Connifarrah said. "I was imprisoned for many years, and when I escaped I was injured. Elyan found me. He is my mate, Brigid. But know I loved your father so very much."

"I know you did." Brigid turned to look at my uncle, then a soft smile lifted her lips. "You are my husband's uncle, sir?"

"I am, my lady," he bowed his head. "Elyan, at your service. But please, if it would be well with you to call me that, I would appreciate it."

Brigid nodded slowly. "I believe I can do that."

"I want you to know, Brigid, your mother searched high and low for you after her memories returned. You can see the scar on her face. It caused her to forget who she was hence her new name. I swear to you, she wanted to find you but your uncle claimed you had died. She mourned you for so long. I believe she would still be mourning you if Finn had not mentioned you during dinner. Only then did she realize you were alive and well."

"I can scarce believe it. I mean, I believe my uncle's treachery. I am pleased he is dust, he does not deserve our thoughts. But I can scarce believe he could do such a farce. You were imprisoned for years, mama."

"I was, my child, but it matters little. Elyan is the very best of males and he has made me very happy."

Tears fell down Brigid's cheeks as she turned to look once more at my uncle.

"I ken I am not your father, Brigid," Elyan started. "And I have no wish to take his place. Conni— Mirren knows this, but I do hope we can get to know each other? I love your mother with all my soul."

Brigid said nothing after a short while. Then, "aye, you are not my father, Elyan. But you are my mother's choice and mate. You are most welcome. And I thank you for saving her life to give us this reunion." She looked over at me. "Can you assist me, my love? I would like to stand."

"Slowly," I begged. She nodded and I helped her. Connifarrah's steady and loving hand guiding us. Once we were all upright, Brigid embraced Elyan and then her mother once more.

"You will dine with us? Stay with us?" she pleaded.

"For as long as you will have us," Elyan offered.

"Won't you need to return to Ireland, Uncle?" I asked.

"Not for some time. And truly, Rexian knows there was a chance I would not return."

"Uncle…" Brigid repeated what I called Elyan. "If all right with you, Elyan, I would like to call you that? It seems more familial than calling you by your given name."

For a split moment, I thought I caught tears in Elyan's eyes. The male was emotional at her request.

"I would be honored to be your uncle, Brigid," he said, his voice soft.

"Good," Brigid grinned, then with a look at me, took her mother's hand and walked ahead of us toward the keep. Elyan stepped up beside me as we watched them walk on.

"Our mates," Elyan sighed.

"Our wives," I agreed.

"They both are truly amazing females."

"They are, Uncle and I am pleased you are with us. Don't

tell Rexian or Raeghar but you were always my favorite."

Elyan tipped his head back and laughed.

Chapter Fourteen

Cahal

Sybine escorted me to my... *our* room as soon as we left the bailey. I was surprised by her ardent affection and welcome home. She was acting more like the lass I knew years ago versus the mother of three and a widow... but then, she was not a widow any longer.

Though I knew her intention, I had to stop her. There was too much that remained unsaid between us. Bearcbhan's face from my dream flashed before my eyes and I pulled on her hand gently.

We were halfway up the spiral stone back staircase when she stopped and looked at me.

"Is something wrong, Cahal?" she asked.

It was the third time in but a couple minutes she had used my name and it gave me pause. Worried she was trying to atone for saying Bearcbhan's name while we started to make love a few days ago, I took her hand and kissed it.

"You honored me with your welcome, Sybine," I said. "But this is not necessary."

Her face fell. "Did you not... want... me?"

"Of course I want you." I stepped up one more step, still two down from her, but we were eye to eye and I cupped her face. "I have always wanted you. I simply want to give you a chance to pause. This is not needed to welcome me back properly. I appreciate it, but you donnae have to."

She placed a finger against my lips and held my gaze. "I want to show you how much I still love you, Cahal. I need you to know that although I mourn Bearcbhan, he is no longer my mate. You are. And though you may think I consider this a duty, I can assure you, it is not. It is a pleasure."

Take Sybine as your true mate, Cahal. You have my blessing to be with her which is more than I asked of you when I took her. I heard Bearcbhan's words in my mind.

I pulled her fingers down from my lips and held them in my hand. "Then, my mate, I thank you for the gift you want to give me. I accept."

Her eyes lit with a sort of fire and happiness sprung to their depths. With a lighter heart than I had had in a while, I followed her up to our chamber and barred the door. Turning to find her, she stood by the sideboard table, a glass of whisky in her hand. She offered it to me and then pushed me down into the chair that faced the fire. The fire burned with her iridescent flame. She said nothing as she knelt and produced a linen, wet with water from our pitcher and basin on the table near the window. Meticulously, she swiped the cloth along my calves and feet, having caught mud and grime from shifting in the bailey after a drizzly rain.

I watched her with a sort of dull arousal and fascination. She was truly treating me to a warrior's welcome. We dragons did not wish our mates to be lowered to a standard not befitting their station. They were the strongest of us all. I had seen males whimper over a splinter in their finger while our females carried our whelps to term and went through the rigors of bearing them only to be fit as before a few days later. It was the female who produced a strong male, and we all knew it and lauded them for it. Males would wash their mate's hair for them after they labored as a show of appreciation and adoration. So for my mate to be washing my feet was a show of love and commitment.

When she was finished, she walked past me to our bed. I caught the faint whiff of rosewater on her skin, and it made me smile. I always did love her scent. Languidly, I looked back to see what she was doing and watched as she pulled down the bed furs and linens and lit some candles nearby.

"I ken this is not our first night together," she said softly as she walked back to me and lowered onto my lap. "But to me, it is the night we pledge to each other. You are my true mate, Cahal MacKay. And I will spend my lifetime proving my love to you."

"And I will spend mine showing you what you mean to me and how much I cherish you. I love you, Sybine. I always have and I always will."

"I know," she kissed me softly but pulled back before more could be done. "And have nae fear I will remind you of it often and make sure you donnae stop showing me how much you love me." The twinkle in her eye made me chuckle.

"Och aye you have my permission to kick my arse if I ever make you doubt it."

"Good," she grinned. "Because you see, we females are fiercely loyal to our males. So you better understand, Cahal, I will nae take it lightly if a female so much as turns your head. You are mine."

Laughing, I set the whisky down and squeezed her to me. "I did not doubt it for a moment. You have a will of fire."

"A what?"

"Finn and I heard the term over in Ireland when speaking of strong females and I couldn't stop thinking of you."

"Well, my mate, this strong female wants you in her bed."

"That is a place I would be happy to be."

"Welcome back, Cahal"

"Welcome back to me Sybine."

I pulled her close and kissed her deeply. She pressed herself to me and held on as I stood. Walking to the bed, I intended to show my true mate how much she meant to me for the rest of our lives.

Cahal

Three months later

inn paced in the Great Hall like a caged dragon.

Brigid's cries echoed down to us and with each one, Finn's fists shook. I could hear our mother, her mother, Sybine, and our healer coaxing and soothing her. After three long hours after Brigid's pains began, Sybine came down to give us an update that everything seemed to be progressing well, but the whelp was far from being ready to deliver. That was five hours ago.

"What in the name of the gods is taking so damn long?" Finn snarled.

"It isn't instant, son," da' said from the chair by the fire. He played with his grandchildren. "All will be well."

238

One of the twins, Adair I believe, it was still hard for me to tell them apart, walked over to me and crawled up onto my lap.

"Uncle Caal," his little voice tried to pronounce my name. But I grinned as I heard it. It was a name he gave me and I loved it.

"What is it, son?" I asked.

"When mama has our little brother or sister, will she make as much noise?"

I breathed a laugh. Sybine had just told me of our expectation two weeks ago and we had announced it just before Brigid's pains began.

"I am nae sure, lad," I said. "Your mother has had you and your brother and sister before. Auntie Brigid hasn't had a whelp. It usually is more difficult for the first one."

Another cry came from above and Finn seethed. I watched him, then turned my attention back on my nephew.

"But you do ken all will be well, aye? Auntie Brigid will be fine."

He nodded his head vigorously. "Aye, it's just really loud."

"Aye lad, it is that," I agreed. "But just think of all the fun you will have when your cousin is born!"

He beamed at that. "Aye, Brogan and I already have a name picked out."

"Oh?" I asked. "Usually it's the parents who name their whelp."

"I ken. Daddy named me," he said softly and my heart

hurt for him. But in the way that children have, he took a single moment to be sad then bounced on my knee. "But Auntie Brigid said we can call him whatever we wanted as long as it is respectful since he'll be our king."

"Your auntie knows best then," I agreed.

A squalid babe's cry split the silence and we all let out a sigh of relief. Finn sagged so much Kai raced for him and held him up. They were both white as a linen sheet throughout the sounds Brigid made. Tahra was advancing well with her whelp and would be delivered in a few months. Kai was ecstatic when they announced but seeing how pale he was and noticing the beads of sweat rolling down his forehead, he was petrified of hearing his mate's screams.

"Thank the gods," Finn kept muttering over and over again. He hurried to the stair.

"Wait, Finn. Shouldn't be long now, son," da' called. "They'll want to clean both the whelp and Brigid then come down to get you. Give them this time."

"But..."

"I ken how you are feeling, lad. I remember it like it was yesterday," Da' encouraged. "But you must allow them this time. If something was happening that needed you, they would come for you."

Finn took a deep breath and held it. He was torn. Wanting to race up the steps to his mate, but also following our father's advice. I couldn't imagine how he must feel and though I kenned I would be feeling it soon, I thanked my luck that Sybine had been through it before.

Finn went back to pacing as I crouched down to set Adair next to his brother and sister. Sitting cross-legged, I picked up one of the little dragon figurines da' had made for the boys and started to pretend to fly it high above the "battle" they were playing. I had just gotten the lads to laugh uproariously and Elowyn to squeal with delight when the sound of another scream pierced the air.

Whipping my eyes to Finn, he blanched and, ignoring our father's advice, raced up the stairs two at a time. Something was happening. I looked over at my father who looked less certain than earlier. Kai fell into the seat I had forfeited and poured a large glass of whisky.

"Dear gods, I..." he began. "I donnae ken if I am strong enough to hear Tahra scream like that."

"It is never easy," da' agreed. "Even after four sons, I worried for my mate when she labored with Tahra."

Another scream split the air. I looked at the boys who were glancing back and forth between the stairs and each other. They were clearly scared. Elowyn was too young to understand but I noticed tears in her eyes and her little lip wobbled. I opened my arms to her and she crawled into them. I held her to my chest and hummed. The boys followed their sister's lead and crawled to me, placing their heads on my legs using me as a pillow.

"It's all right," I soothed and hummed some more.

Soon, after two more cries from Brigid, we heard another squalling cry.

The boys lifted their heads, huge smiles on their faces, looked at each other and, "Twins!" they cried.

And I had never been happier in my life.

The End

Acknowledgements

Thank you to all my fans who have enjoyed the DragonFire series! I am so very excited to share Cahal's and Sybine's story with you! It has taken a lot longer than I was expecting and hoping to get this story completed, but I am very proud of how it turned out!

Be sure to keep an eye out for the third and maybe final installment Born of Fire coming 2022-2023! It is a modern take on the series. I am looking forward to working on it!

As always, I would love it if you would write a review on your favorite book review site and follow me on social media under the handles M. Katherine Clark Author. Be sure to sign up for my newsletter on my website; www.mkatherineclark.net for the latest information on new releases!

www.ingramcontent.com/pod-product-compliance
Lightning Source LLC
Chambersburg PA
CBHW052030020726
47501CB00004B/1349